WANTED

A Bird Blacker Bounty-Hunter Mystery

T. I. ALVARADO

*Dedicated to the toughest dames I've ever known.
To Maria, who fought tooth and nail to come to this land
just so we could have a decent life. And to my Nina,
who packed it all up and followed me across the
country so that we may start a new life of our own.
I love you both, forever and for true.*

Manufactured in the United States of America.

ISBN 978-0-7394-7050-3

Cover design by Amy Martin.

DEMON BEAST OF KOREATOWN

IT'S RIDICULOUSLY EASY TO get a man naked; not much effort is required at all. He'll doff on a dare or if there's money to be made or if he's drunk, but most of all a man will veritably leap out of his clothes at the slightest possibility of sex, regardless of potential consequences. In fact, it's a wonder all men's clothing doesn't come standard with quick-release Velcro straps.

And so it was that Harold Stiffe found himself wearing only boxers and tied to a chair in the middle of his dingy bedroom. A small forty-watt lamp by the bedside provided just enough illumination to discern markings on his body. Tattoos running up and down both arms testified to the biker's deep-rooted love of all things Harley-Davidson as well as to his many years on the mean streets. Unfortunately, sometimes there are things meaner than the streets, and tonight he'd invited one of them right into his home. As a result his face was beaten red and raw as hamburger.

A hand delicately caressed his bruised face. One finger, long and graceful, glided along the line of his jaw. "Honey, just tell me where the money is. I have a tight schedule. I can't fool around all night."

The sneering biker looked up, no fear in his eyes. "I thought

this was just foreplay. When are we getting to the good stuff?"
A cocky bastard, his smile was arrogant and lascivious.

"Suit yourself."

Smack! A hand struck him across the face. Stiffe barely
flinched.

"That the best you can do?" His grin showed nicotine-
stained teeth.

"Oh, no, sugar. This is."

The graceful hand balled up into an iron fist, and—Pow!—
hit with the force of a sledgehammer. The blow knocked the
chair back on two legs. It hung there for a second, teetering,
then slammed back down and snapped Stiffe's head forward.

"How was that—good for you?"

He took a moment to compose himself, the smile still there
but a lot less smug. He swished around something in his mouth,
then spat out blood and a yellow tooth.

"You . . . you hit like a man."

His tormentor was in fact a woman—beautiful, exotic, and
dangerous, she was like a swaying cobra just before it strikes
and fills your veins with venom. She wore only a red lace bra
and panties, because that's what men like, isn't it—red? Her
defined muscles glistened with sweat from working over the
biker's face for half the night.

"Sweet-talker," she said as she cleaned Stiffe's blood from
her fist with a discarded T-shirt. She ran her hand across his
face once more. She was alternating between brutal blows and
gentle strokes, and he didn't know when to flinch. But she
underestimated him and brought her hand too close to that
cocky smile of his. In a split second he jerked forward and
clamped his teeth down on her palm.

Surprisingly, the woman did not cry out in pain. She did
try to pull her hand free, though not in panic, not in fear. "Let

go," she commanded with a stern voice and a frosty stare. She looked down at him as one would a slug found crawling across a dinner plate—disgusting, unwanted, and beneath contempt.

He did not release her. Instead, he bit down harder on her hand, breaking the skin, drawing blood. The smirk had returned, through the flesh he gripped in his teeth, as he looked up at her.

"Bad dog." The strike was surprising in its speed and control, especially considering how much pain she must have been in. She cracked him exactly in the spot where jawbone hinged to cranium. Not only did he lose his grip on her hand, he almost lost his entire lower jaw.

She took the dirty shirt and cleaned the blood from her wounded hand. Once clean, she could assess the damage: a row of teeth marks lined the top of her right hand, just below the knuckles. For the first time that evening, she lost her cool. She grabbed his hair and violently wrenched his head. "You better not have anything," she snarled right in his ear as she pulled his head back at an unnatural angle.

With his head bent to such an extreme Stiffe could do little more than grunt in response. She'd snap his neck if she kept pulling, and there was no indication that she planned to stop. A wet gurgle escaped his lips, his face red with the strain.

Suddenly, a loud thumping caught his tormentor's attention. The bathroom door a few feet behind rattled noisily. Someone was slamming against it from the other side trying to break out. The wood was old but still strong enough to hold up to the beating.

"Your little pal wants to come out and play," she said as she eyed the door. She released Stiffe's hair, sending his head flopping forward.

He gasped and sputtered, then warned her, "Leave him out of

this, you crazy bitch." There was genuine concern in his voice.

"I'd be more worried about myself, if I were you." She wrapped the shirt around her wounded hand. "Now, where is Mr. V's money?"

"That's my money and you know it! I ain't givin' you one single fucking dime! Not one, you bitch! I'm gonna rip your head off and crap in your skull, you hear me?" He strained against the ropes, eyes bulging, spittle flying in every direction.

The woman seemed neither impressed nor particularly worried by his passionate display. She smiled and shook her head disapprovingly, as if dealing with a petulant child who was not getting his way.

"Well, come on then, tough guy, go on and bust out of those ropes," she taunted. "Get out of the jam your dick got you into."

He pulled and strained against his bonds, but of course he couldn't break them. When it came to subduing opponents, she knew her way around a knot—she knew her way around several kinds of knots, actually.

"My employer has some unforeseen legal bills. You know how expensive lawyers can be. He's done favors for you. So consider this . . . a contribution."

"He can pay for his own damned lawyer, and you can go straight to hell." He spat at his oppressor in one last act of defiance. He was surprised when she quickly sidestepped and easily dodged the glob. His surprise was even greater when she whipped out a gun from under a pile of her clothes and aimed the weapon at his head.

"Last chance, you dumb ape—the money," she said, once again cool, once again fully in control.

The biker flinched at first but quickly regained his composure. "Lady, you're forgetting one fundamental element of this situation . . . " He leered at her body, drinking in every inch from bra down to panties. "You don't have the balls."

She pressed the cold silencer against his forehead. Then she smiled and said . . .

"I don't need them."

A sudden gun flash was the last thing Stiffe ever saw.

•

Ladybird "Bird" Blacker hated wearing the Kevlar vest required for her job. Even when she was a police officer, the bulletproof vest was a cumbersome inconvenience. Still, it saved her life a few times, and now that she spent her days chasing down bail jumpers as a bounty hunter, it was one of the few things she could count on for backup. The attractive thirty year old strapped the vest around her torso, careful not to wrinkle her meticulously ironed shirt or sensible tie. After all, take care of your clothes, and they'll take care of you, she always said.

The same high standards held true for her body, with a runner's build she maintained by running three miles every other day—it used to be every day in her twenties, but, well, age slows us all. A tight ponytail pulled back her jet-black hair, one of many features courtesy of her Hispanic mother. Her piercing green eyes were the only inheritance her Irish father had left her.

Bird sat in the passenger side of an old Ford van parked in a rundown Los Angeles neighborhood just north of Koreatown, where the police choppers flew thick as mosquitoes every night. The Ford's paint job had seen better days, but it had enough shine left that it was obvious the owner took care of the vehicle. Inside, only the two front seats remained, everything in the rear having been gutted long ago to make room for uncooperative passengers. Every time Bird moved in her seat, the van squeaked underneath. "Jesse, I told you to get the suspension fixed," she admonished.

In the driver's seat slouched Jesse, Bird's "partner." More of a nuisance most of the time, she kept him around because, after all, it was his van. "I will, man. Soon as we bag this guy. No tengo dinero, know what I mean?"

Jesse's financial status was obvious, from the raggedy T-shirts he loved to buy at thrift stores to the same pair of sandals he'd worn since Bird could remember. Hell, he even got girlfriends to cut his hair for free. This produced mixed results, as evidenced by the shaggy nest currently atop the twenty-something's head.

How Jesse kept getting girlfriends was beyond Bird's understanding. He was six feet tall but looked shorter because he slouched so much. He hardly ever shaved. And though he would go on and on about yoga, one could hardly call his body athletic. Then there was his complete inability to tan . . . Maybe that's what straight girls were into these days—scruffy, pasty guys with bad posture. He certainly wouldn't have been Bird's first choice.

Bird shook her head in general disapproval, then went back to inspecting her equipment. She checked each of her bullets, one by one, before sliding them into a gun magazine. She held one up to her eyes, transfixed. It wasn't that she was a gun nut or had some sort of bullet fetish. She simply appreciated the efficiency of the ammunition—it did exactly what it was designed to do, and did it well. "Precise. Perfect. Professional. Unlike some people." She looked at Jesse out of the corner of her eye.

Oblivious, Jesse struggled with his own Kevlar vest, the van's suspension squealing every time he jerked around.

"People are gonna think we're making out in here." She frowned at her twitchy partner.

"Would that be so terrible?" Jesse puckered his lips.

"Not in your most desperate dreams," she quickly retorted. Then Bird noticed Jesse's empty holster. "Hold up there. Where's your gun?"

"I told you, Bird," he sighed, as if explaining the obvious. "We go in waving guns around, all we're gonna get is hostility in return."

"We are fugitive-recovery agents," she said, holding up her gun. "This little machine is tool, partner, and best friend. We don't leave home without it."

"Best friend? Dude, it's a ninety-dollar Chinese knockoff. You should try making friends with people instead."

Twenty minutes into a case and he's already raising my blood pressure, Bird thought as she stared at Jesse's smiling face. "Listen to me," she said slowly. "This perp is wanted for manslaughter." She waited for the information to sink in, but Jesse just kept smiling serenely. It was infuriating! "Look, you're carrying a gun even if I have to shove it up your rectum. End of discussion."

"OK," Jesse relented, "but I still say it's a spiritual mistake." He pulled out his gun from a duffel bag. "Rectum," he tittered.

Bird and Jesse carefully walked around a street corner and made their way toward a particularly dilapidated house. They never parked directly in front of a skip's home—that sort of thing only made bail jumpers skittish and prone to running out the back.

Once at the porch, they saw a bug zapper hanging overhead, crackling with the night's slaughter of countless insects. Stupid bugs, Bird thought. Don't even have the sense to stay away from something that's going to get them killed. For some reason, the thought gave her pause.

Next to her, Jesse stared forlornly as the zapper cut short

another misguided bug's life. "That could've been someone's mother in a past life," he said, shaking his head. "It was already a little moth's mother." He reached up to unhook the zapper.

Bird grabbed him, pulled him back. "Pay attention. Here's how it's going down—I go in through here." She pointed at the front door. "You stay in the backyard, make sure he doesn't sneak out. Clear?"

Jesse nodded, scratching absentmindedly at his vest, then paused. "What if—"

"Good." Bird pushed him off the porch. "Off you go."

Jesse stumbled away in the dark and tripped. "Ow, my foot bone," he said as he rounded the corner.

Bird rolled her eyes, a common response when dealing with Jesse, then tried the front door—locked, and set up with what looked like three Deadbolt locks. Wow, this guy's a real security nut. Fortunately, there's one thing all nuts have in common: they can be cracked. Bird tried a nearby window—the glass pane moved as she pushed up on it. Three Deadbolts and the moron leaves his window open. She smiled. This was going to be easier than she thought.

Unlike Bird's previous job in law enforcement, as a bounty hunter she didn't need a warrant to enter a bail jumper's home. Many states don't even license bounty hunters, figuring if someone wants to run around tracking down criminals, well, that's less work for the already overworked police. In essence, that means bounty hunting is like having a baby—any schmuck with the right equipment can do it.

While some bounty hunters (or "fugitive-recovery agents") preferred to first knock and announce themselves loudly before breaking down the door, Bird had found that the more stealthy she was when on a case, the less she tended to get shot at. Always a good thing.

Once through the house window, Bird dusted herself off, paused, dusted off again, and was about to walk away . . . but she couldn't help it; gritting her teeth in resignation, she dusted herself off one last time.

A perfunctory search revealed an empty first floor. Of course, this didn't mean her target wasn't hiding down here somewhere—Bird once found a bail jumper stuffed in a two-foot-tall clothes hamper, under a sink—but this particular skip didn't know she was here, which meant he was probably lying somewhere watching TV. Instead of cramming himself inside one.

She gripped the wobbly banister to go to the second floor but stopped in her tracks when she saw it was covered with grime. "Place is a deathtrap. A filthy deathtrap." She sighed and wiped her hand.

Suddenly, silently, a gun reached out of the inky darkness behind her. The female assassin held the weapon right up to the back of Bird's oblivious head. She was about to paint the walls red with the inside of Bird's skull, when the back door suddenly swung open. As Jesse ambled in, the killer fell back into the shadows before anyone could detect her.

"Hey, man, back door was open," Jesse announced.

"Shh," Bird whispered, finger to her lips. "He'll hear us. I told you to stay out back."

"Oh, right." Jesse crouched down, trying to be inconspicuous. "Should I . . . ?" He pointed to the back door.

"Yes, go." Bird shooed him away. "And keep both eyes open."

"I always do, man. I'm like a hawk. Nothing escapes my sight." He bugged out his eyes to emphasize his birdlike eyesight. Neither of them noticed as a shadow moved in the darkness behind them.

When Bird reached the second floor, just as quiet and gloomy as the first, she noticed a door with dim light pooling out from under it. This was it; her bail jumper was probably in there. Fortunately, Bird still had the element of surprise. But she had to move fast, before the guy had a chance to react, and that meant . . . I finally get to kick in a door! she thought with glee. Just like on every cop show I ever loved. I've been waiting years for this. Gripping the gun with both hands, she lifted her right leg dramatically—it was such perfect form that T. J. Hooker himself would be proud.

Still, something nagged at her, and leg still in the air Bird reached down to try the doorknob—it was open. No need to kick in the door. Nuts, she thought, as she lowered her leg. No cop-show moment for her. Instead, Bird rushed into the room, her gun leading the way. "Harold Stiffe, I got a warrant for your arrest."

There was no movement; the room was silent as death. In fact, Bird thought the place was empty, until she noticed the silhouette of someone sitting in a chair. A small, greasy table lamp was knocked over in a corner of the room. Bird's instincts told her this was her man. "Harry, get your butt off the chair and your hands in the air," she demanded, gun trained on him.

No response from the figure.

"Got wax in your ears? I will shoot your criminal ass."

Again, not a twitch from the man.

Great, another one of those hardened seen-it-all types. In Bird's experience, these were the worst skips to deal with, because pointing a gun at them had about as much effect as pointing a finger. Usually, they'd already been through so much in prison that nothing on the outside scared them anymore, except the prospect of going back in.

Fine, we'll do it the hard way then, Bird thought confidently. After all, she was a fugitive-recovery professional, and there was little she couldn't handle. "I'll take no shit from you, Stiffe." She kept the gun aimed at the figure, while feeling around the wall for a light switch with her free hand. "I'm armed and dangerous." A reassuring click filled the room with light.

Harold Stiffe, in nothing but boxers, sat tied to the chair, his face red and puffy, a bullet hole right between his open, glassy eyes.

"Jeez, Stiffe, who'd you piss off?" Bird asked the dead man. She was suddenly a whole lot less confident as a cold realization sent shivers down her spine: what if the killer was still there?

A sudden thump, thump, thump shook a door across the room, and Bird nearly jumped out of her skin. She pointed her gun at the door. "Come out with your hands up!"

But the door had decided to clam up—no more thumping and no one coming out to surrender.

"I said come out!"

When no one answered, Bird carefully walked to the side of the door, slowly turned the knob, and swung it open. She sucked in a deep breath, then filled the doorway with her frame, legs spread, gun held firmly in both hands. She used her best don't-fuck-with-me glare. What she saw in the bathroom wiped it right off her face.

The creature vaguely resembled a dog—that is, it had four legs and a tail, but it was so large, so unbelievably huge, that perhaps Bird was staring down something prehistoric, something that hunted mastodons with impunity in times long past. All muscle and teeth, it was big enough to give pit bulls nightmares. And now the nightmare creature charged right at the woman who had invaded its territory.

"Lord, help—" Bird breathed just before the canine locomotive barged into her, knocking her clean across the bedroom. She got off a shot that broke a window, then promptly lost her gun. In less than a second she was blasted out of the bedroom, into the hallway outside.

•

In the backyard, Jesse heard a loud bang, followed by tinkling and what seemed like a crystalline waterfall falling before him. He looked down to see glass shards by his feet, then up at the broken second-story window. It took a moment before he could formulate the proper response. "Hey, you need help up there, Bird . . . ? Hello?"

•

In the second-floor hallway, Bird held back the huge dog with her bare hands, gripping tightly at its jowls and the folds of skin around its neck. All she could see were jaws snapping and snarling inches from her face. One thought looped over and over through her mind: what a stupid way to die. Her back hit the banister, and it creaked under the combined weight of dog and woman as they pushed against the ancient wood.

"Get off me!" she yelled.

"Hey, man, what are you doing to the dog?" Jesse looked on curiously from the first floor.

"Shoot it!" Bird screamed, pushing back the growling thing's head, so close now she could smell its breath.

"What?" Jesse said incredulously. "I'm not shooting a helpless dog. What's wrong with you, man?"

"It's going to eat my face, you idiot!" She bobbed and weaved her head to avoid the snapping teeth, then somehow she found the strength to shove the dog a few feet away.

"Look, man, just show him you're not a threat. Let him know you're friendly, and he'll back down."

The dog stood in the hallway between Bird and the stairway down, blocking any possible escape. Her arms felt like lead, and she knew she wouldn't be able to hold off another attack. "Nice hellhound," she said with a forced grin. "I'm your friend."

The dog leaned down low, its muscles tensing visibly. A low, guttural snarl quickly built up to a rumble Bird could feel through the floorboards. It wasn't backing down; it was getting ready to rush at her.

"Jesus, shoot the dog! Shoot the dog!" she said, panicking.

In a split second, it leaped and slammed her against the banister. The canine bit into Bird's chest, ripping out a chunk of her Kevlar vest. Suddenly, a loud snap announced the railing had had enough of all this nonsense. The wood shattered, sending Bird and the dog plummeting to the first floor, where they landed with a splintering crack.

The dog whimpered, dazed and wobbly from the fall. But at least it had lost interest in Bird. For the moment.

Bird curled up into a fetal position, the wind knocked out of her worse than that time in sixth grade when she fell off the monkey bars—possibly the single most embarrassing moment of her life. She had been trying to get the attention of the most popular girl in school by doing a handstand on top of the metal framework. The girl would see Bird's acrobatics and instantly fall for the tomboy, and thus Bird would win a sweet first kiss from her schoolgirl crush. Instead, the young Bird lost her balance and fell like a narcoleptic monkey off a tree limb. In place of a kiss, Bird got a mouthful of sand as she wheezed for breath on the ground. So, no romance—on the other hand, that may well have been the day she lost her virginity, since she hit one of the steel tubes rather hard on the way down. At least Bird's two-story plunge this time was only a matter of life and death.

"Shoot . . . dog," she found enough breath to whisper.

"I—I can't do it, Bird," Jesse said regretfully. "Don't ask me to."

"You . . . hippie . . . bastard." She glared at him, then felt around for something to use as a weapon. She knew full well that thing wouldn't stay dazed for long.

Fearlessly, Jesse walked up to the pony-size dog and held out his empty palms. "Hey, boy, you OK? I won't hurt you, man. Yeah, you're a good boy, aren't you?"

The canine growled as Jesse neared.

But he continued undeterred. "Feel my vibes, dude. I'm a friend. Understand?" he said in a soothing voice, then began a low chant—"Ohm, ohm, ohm"—as he placed both hands under the animal's jaws. The dog sniffed at Jesse's palms, stopped growling, then licked the hands playfully. "Did the crazy lady scare you?" Jesse asked in a tone of voice reserved for children who've scraped a knee. "Yes, she's a mean old lady, isn't she? Yes she is. There's no joy in her heart, is there? No there isn't, no there isn't." He rubbed the dog's ears.

Bird couldn't believe her eyes—the fearsome beast that nearly took her head off was now little more than a lapdog. As the breath returned to her lungs, so did her anger. "Why didn't you just shoot?" she asked through gritted teeth.

"He was just protecting his home. Besides," Jesse paused and rubbed at his unkempt hair, "I couldn't shoot him."

"Then you must want me dead, just as I always suspected. Do you hate me, Jesse, is that it?" she asked with resignation. It wouldn't be the first time a partner had wanted her dead.

"No, you don't understand."

"Enlighten me, goddamn it," she said, still sitting on the floor.

"I couldn't shoot because . . . well, I got no bullets in my gun, OK? I threw them away."

Unsure of what she'd just heard, Bird shook her head, then twirled a finger in her ear. "You didn't just say . . . You threw your bullets away?"

"See, I figured it out," Jesse said proudly. "Guns don't kill people. Bullets going really, really fast do."

Bird looked down at the shredded vest that had barely kept her heart from being ripped out. She saw the monster that had attacked her, sitting at Jesse's feet, getting its ears rubbed, and not, as she would have preferred, mounted and stuffed above a fireplace. "He threw them away," she said, shaking her head in disbelief.

As Bird pulled off the ruined Kevlar from her chest, her face contorted in disgust. She noticed a slimy substance covering her hand. "What is that?" A quick sniff confirmed her fears. "Aw, dog snot, all over my linen shirt!" Her favorite shirt, as a matter of fact. The one she had worn today only because it was laundry day and everything else was dirty. "You'd better hope I don't find my gun. Swear to God I'll shoot the both of you filthy animals." She pointed an accusatory finger at Jesse.

"Bird, don't, you'll upset him again." The dog's bowel-shaking growl was a pretty good sign she had done just that, and its bared canine fangs were a dead giveaway.

"Jesse," she said nervously, "hold onto that animal."

"I'm trying." Jesse gripped the powerful neck, but was losing ground fast. "You should've just been nice."

"Oh, crap!" Bird jumped to her feet and quickly ran to a door just behind her. Of course it was locked, and of course the dog was about to break free from Jesse's grip and attack her once more. On the bright side, she finally had her chance to kick in a door like they did on TV—she knocked it open on the first try using one foot and about a quart of adrenaline racing through her body. No sooner was she on the other side than the beast was loose and charging.

"Madre de Dios!" she exclaimed in her mother's tongue as the monster battered the door open and knocked her aside. Only her fear-fueled grip on the doorknob kept her from flying off. And fortunately for her, it was a basement door. The animal flew past, then tumbled down a flight of stairs, giving Bird ample time to rush back out and slam the door shut behind her. She quickly removed her tie, looped it around the doorknob, and tied the other end to a nearby table leg. Then she fell on hands and knees and heaved, from fear, from the physical impact of falling off the banister, and, last but certainly not least, from finding a corpse with a bullet in its head.

So preoccupied were Jesse and Bird that they did not notice the female figure watching them from the inky shadows of the dilapidated house. They did not notice the figure seemingly checking out Bird's ass as she got up from throwing up on the floor. And they definitely did not notice the mysterious figure smile wryly just before sinking back into the darkness.

THE OTHER DA VINCI

WHILE SOME HIGHLY SUCCESSFUL businesses could afford to line their office walls with works of art by your more famous modern masters (a Pollock in the reception area, a Warhol in the executive washroom), there was only one business in the Los Angeles area that could boast of at least a dozen original Da Vinci paintings in the building. Each one had been lovingly crafted by the one and only Vicky Da Vinci, full-time head of Da Vinci Bail Bonds—and part-time artist. For a while, the brassy forty-something with a thick New York accent had even claimed to be a distant relative of that "other" Da Vinci. But this inevitably led to much hearty laughter from everyone she told, so she no longer mentioned it. Besides, her work was strong enough to stand on its own, without comparison to that of artists long dead.

Even now she sat at her cluttered desk, brush in hand, tongue stuck out, eyes squinting, as she dabbed at her latest masterpiece—a colorful canvas that, for lack of a better description, could be classified as abstract. "Where are they?" she said as she painted. "What is so confusing about 'Call me the second you find the skip'?"

"Why don't you try to relax?" said Dippo, her receptionist. His own desk, about ten feet away from Vicky, was as organized as hers was messy.

"Because the fate of fifty thousand dollars of my money is

on the line, that's why," Vicky said, then tossed the paintbrush into a bucket under her desk.

"They haven't let you down yet."

"Let's just say I'm still a bit surprised every time they come back alive."

A loud squeal outside signaled the arrival of Bird and Jesse, the van lurching to a stop in front of the office window.

"And they bucked the odds again," Vicky said. She pulled away from her desk to reveal that she was in a wheelchair. She handled it expertly, like it was a part of her body and not something life had forced upon her.

Bird shuffled in through the front door, disheveled, shirt untucked, and, of course, dog slobber smattered all over her. She was perhaps not a broken woman but certainly not a happy one either. In contrast, Jesse followed close behind, smiling benignly, not a care in the world.

"What took you so long?" Vicky asked gruffly.

"I'm fine, thanks," Bird said.

"Did you find Stiffe?"

"He came along real quiet. But his best friend put up quite a struggle."

Vicky rolled to the window and stared at the old vehicle outside. "Is he in the van?"

"He's in the freezer," Bird said and walked over to the office assistant. "Dippo, I feel some major bruises coming on. You got any ice around here? Something cold?"

Dippo glanced forlornly at Vicky and sighed. "Try her heart," he muttered.

"Freezer? What are you prattling about?" Vicky rolled right up to Bird and glared. "Where's Harold Stiffe?"

"Stiffe's a stiff. Someone plugged him right between the eyes."

Vicky leaned back and considered this. "So you found him, right?"

"You know I always get my man."

"That means I get my bond money back!" she exclaimed joyfully.

"Vicky, I found a dead body. Then a mutant dog almost ripped me apart." Bird rubbed at her aching back. "This thing was a monster—a Clydesdale with razors for teeth! I'm having serious career doubts here."

"Yes, that does sound troublesome," Vicky said dismissively and rolled to Dippo's desk. "Do you have the Billy Veach file?"

Dippo handed her a folder.

"Thank you, love," she said, causing Dippo to smile ever so slightly.

"Maybe you didn't hear me," Bird insisted. "A dead body and a killer dog. Both in the same day."

"Bird, we all feel your pain," Vicky said. "Right, Dippo?"

"Sure, I hurt." He shrugged.

"Jesse?" Vicky asked.

"I think His Holiness the Dalai Lama put it best when—"

Vicky quickly cut him off. "There, see?" she said smugly. "Now, let's get on to the business at hand. I have another skip for you. Follow me, please." She rolled into her private office, leaving Bird with no chance to protest. Three unfinished canvases stood against the walls of the room, one door led to a small bathroom, and another door served as the rear exit.

Vicky leafed through the file Dippo had given her. "The perp skipped on a tax-fraud charge. He shouldn't be much trouble for a pro like you."

"That's what you said about Stiffe." Bird pulled at her soiled shirt. I'm sure dog slobber stains, she thought. I should make her pay for the dry cleaning. Yet Bird knew full well she was more likely to get blood from a stone than to squeeze money from Vicky Da Vinci. She sniffed at the shirt and recoiled instantly. "That dog got me all-all-all filthy," she said. "Can I use your sink?"

"Behind you." Vicky waved.

Bird unbuttoned her shirt, went into the bathroom, and ran the tap. She hoped to God she could get the stink out.

"Look, I'm terribly sorry about your wardrobe," Vicky said with all the sincerity of a lizard. "But this one shouldn't be any problem at all. We're talking tax fraud, after all."

"Al Capone went down for tax fraud." Bird scrubbed at the shirt in the sink. "Besides, I need a vacation."

"The day Bird Blacker can't handle a simple tax dodger, well, that's a dark day in the annals of bounty hunting."

"There are no annals of bounty hunting."

"You're lucky there aren't. You'd never get in them."

"Oh, blow me, OK? I almost died today."

"'Blow me'? That's your best shot?" Vicky tisked. "Maybe you are losing your edge after all."

Bird walked out of the bathroom, wearing a clean but sopping-wet shirt. She got right in Vicky's face. "OK then, how about, 'Blow me vigorously'?"

Jesse poked his head into the office, took one look at Bird's clothing, and said, "Looks like a regular wet T-shirt contest in here." When the only response he got was an angry grunt, he continued, "There's some little girl here to see you."

"I don't hang out with little girls," Bird said.

"Whatever you say, man," he muttered and ducked back out.

"Vicky, I'd like my 10 percent from the Stiffe job," Bird said.

The older woman flinched at the mere mention of having to pay out money. "First tell me you'll do the Veach job."

"I don't know . . ."

"Please, Bird, I implore you! This bond's for $750,000. Don't make me go to Mochabean." She shuddered. "That psychopath will fuck it all up."

"That's not my problem . . . Wait, you're still using Mochabean? Have you lost your mind?" Bird looked around, half expecting to find the man.

"If you won't do the job, what other choice do I have—rise out of this wheelchair and snatch the guy myself? Is that what you want, Bird Blacker?" She lifted herself out of the wheelchair, making sure to exaggerate the strain of the effort. "Now, don't mind if I fall. It's been a while since I've stood on my own legs . . . God, the pain!"

"Oh, stop it, DeNiro. You know, you're worse than my mother with the dramatics."

Vicky dropped back into her chair. "If you won't do the job, it's either me or Mochabean. That's all I got."

"You know that guy's an animal. He gives us all a bad name." Her eyes darted around the room, checking the exits for a quick escape, something she did instinctively whenever the subject of Mochabean came up.

"Yeah, well, you leave me no choice. Besides, he wouldn't be nearly as big a concern if you hadn't done him wrong. Look at you, all twitchy, scared he's going to jump out from every shadow. All because you got greedy."

"That—that's not it at all." Bird furrowed her brow in that petulant way she used to when her mother caught her with her hand in the cookie jar and a face full of crumbs. She couldn't look Vicky in the eye, so instead she concentrated on cleaning the stains on her wet shirt. She tugged on one end of the shirt while she rubbed forcefully at the dirty spots with a handkerchief. "The guy's just trouble. Plenty of brawn, but there's nothing upstairs. What I did to him—OK, yes, it's questionable, but that's ancient history. I just don't want innocent people getting hurt is all. That's exactly what'll happen if you bring him into this. Oh, and just so we're perfectly clear, I am not scared of Mochabean."

Jesse poked his head back in the office. "Yo, man."

"Jesus!" A startled Bird pulled too hard on her shirt and popped off one of the buttons. It zinged across the room and bounced off Vicky's forehead.

"Ah, my eye!" Vicky screamed and covered her face with her hand. "I'm a visual artist, you cretin!"

"Cut it out. It was nowhere near your eye." She wiggled a finger through the hole where her button used to be. "Look at this . . . I hate fixing these."

"This chick won't leave, man," Jesse continued. "Says she's your sister. I told her you don't have a sister, but . . . "

"Oh, no." Bird froze, terror washing over her face.

•

Ruby Blacker was a chipper twenty-year-old in pigtails, with a dazzling smile and the kind of natural, innocent beauty that went out with malt shops. She stood in the middle of Da Vinci Bail Bonds grinning, a small suitcase in each hand. The instant Bird walked in, Ruby's eyes lit up. "Pretty Birdie!"

"What are you doing here?" Bird asked, her words a miasma of suspicion, fear, and dread.

"I went to your apartment, but you weren't there," Ruby said, still smiling. "Your landlord said you hang out here, so, here I am." She dropped her suitcases and rushed to Bird, who drew back for a split second before the smaller girl gripped her in a bear hug and lifted her clean off the ground.

"Hey, can I call you 'Pretty Birdie'?" Jesse asked.

"No, you can't," Bird said after Ruby set her down. "Everyone, this is Ruby . . . my sister."

"Howdy." Ruby beamed. She rocked back and forth on her toes, a possessive arm around her big sister.

Moments later, a frantic Bird gestured wildly as she talked on her cell phone and paced in a corner of the office. She tried to keep her voice down to a whisper—no sense involving the entire office in her personal life—but was failing miserably. "Mom," she whined into the phone, "why didn't you ask me if she could come visit? It's common courtesy. Remember that? Courtesy? That thing you tried for years to drill into my head? Didn't work, by the way."

"So, Ruby, why has Bird never mentioned you?" Vicky asked.

"Oh, you know Bird."

Vicky nodded in agreement, then abruptly stopped. "Actually, not very well, no." She shook her head.

"She did always keep to herself. Maybe that's what makes her such a good PI."

"I beg your pardon, a good what?" Vicky said, confused.

"You know, a sleuth, a gumshoe, private dick."

"Man, Bird's no dick," Jesse piped in. "Not a private one, anyway."

"She's not a detective?" Ruby asked.

"Not as far as any of us is aware, dear," Vicky said.

In the background Bird continued her rant. "It's just, I'm in the middle of a situation here, Mom. I really wish you would have called."

"Oh." Ruby lowered her head in disappointment. "She doesn't call home very often. It's hard to keep track. Last I heard she was going to be a detective."

Bird argued at her cell phone, picturing her mother's

disapproving face on it. "It's just scary here ... No, not *Silence of the Lambs* scary ... Mom, I promise there's no cannibals involved ... Mom ... Mom ... Mom!"

"How long will you be staying?" Vicky asked, and instantly grabbed Bird's attention from across the room.

"Don't you go making any plans," Bird yelled at Ruby, then went back to fighting with the cell phone. Her hands were white, she was gripping it so tightly. "Mom, isn't it enough I send you all that money for her? Now you gotta stick me with the kid too?"

"I'm not a kid," Ruby pouted.

Bird spun her head so fast it was a miracle her neck didn't break. She glared at the intruder, the trespasser whom she was now expected to welcome into her life. They had nothing in common, these two. Nothing except genetics. And there was precious little Bird could do about that.

"All right," she sighed into the cell phone. "How long? A week? Mom, listen to me carefully: not a day longer."

"Really?" Ruby said joyfully. "I can stay? Pretty Birdie, you're the best, no matter what anyone says."

Bird was sure an insult lay in there somewhere, but she was too put-upon to search for it. She had more important things to do, like planning an itinerary full of touristy events (preferably cheap ones) that would distract Ruby for the week. Then she could ship her sister back to Texas and go back to her nice, normal routine, risking her life on a daily basis chasing down bail jumpers.

"Vicky, I'm on vacation for the rest of the week."

"You can't do that to me." Da Vinci was aghast.

"Let's get this over with." Bird gripped Ruby's arm and led her toward the door. "Jesse," she grunted and gestured at the suitcases in the middle of the room. "A gentleman always carries a lady's bags."

"Well, crumpets and tea," he said as he scooped up the luggage. "I'll just put these in your horse-drawn carriage, milady." He gave Ruby a knowing wink as he passed her by.

"Wait." Vicky stopped them at the door. "What am I supposed to do about the Veach job?"

Bird shrugged. "Didn't you say something about getting him yourself?"

"You'll regret this, Bird. Mark my words."

"I regret a lot of things. Add it to my tab."

(3)

CALIFORNIA DREAMING

THE REST OF THE week went about as well as could be expected, if you're the kind of person who usually expects the worst. Fortunately, Bird was just such a person, and she was not disappointed.

On the first day of vacation Ruby coldcocked Superman. Bird had decided to spend the afternoon at the Walk of Fame on Hollywood Boulevard. It was free, aside from parking, and you could see the Hollywood sign from there—it was perfect, combining two Tinseltown landmarks and nicely accommodating Bird's limited budget. It took only a moment's lapse before something went terribly wrong. Bird and Jesse were taking pictures of their feet standing in the cement footprints of Darth Vader and C3-PO in front of Mann's Chinese Theatre. By the time Bird noticed her sister had wandered off, it was too late. She could see Ruby in the distance arguing with one of the many people who dress up as famous characters and hang out in front of the theater. For a fee, tourists can get their picture taken with Marilyn Monroe, Spider-Man, or a myriad of other real and fictional individuals. Ruby had not known about the fee and didn't seem pleased when the overweight Superman, his gut peeking out from under the blue spandex, demanded fifteen dollars for having photographed him. Heated words were exchanged, he placed a menacing hand on Ruby's shoulder, and before Bird could intervene, the chunky champion found himself flat on his back with a swollen eye. So much for being faster than a speeding bullet.

They made themselves scarce before the bike cops arrived, but that incident set the benchmark for Ruby's visit to L.A. The day usually started out promising, then everything went terribly wrong. For example . . .

On the second day Jesse almost drowned off the Santa Monica Pier. He got to arguing with a fisherman about "fish's rights" and ended up in the drink for his trouble. Bird jumped in to save him, reluctantly, and ruined another outfit. Turns out seaweed stains.

On the third day Bird tumbled down the side of a cliff. She was so busy keeping an eye on both her wayward charges as they strolled along Runyan Canyon in the Hollywood Hills that she didn't watch her own step. And over and down and over and under and sideways she went. Fortunately, an aspiring model/actress out walking her dog broke Bird's fall. And possibly a femur.

The fourth day began with a discussion about whether to go to Disneyland, as Ruby wanted, or find a more economical pastime, like at a nice city park, as Bird insisted. Multilateral talks about the commercialization of American entertainment and the abuse of power by people who happened to be in authority simply because they were born first soon deteriorated into a screaming match about whose ass looked bigger in jeans. Even after Bird relented to Ruby's choice, they spent hours stuck on L.A.'s notoriously congested freeways on the way to Anaheim. By the time they arrived at Disneyland it was thirty minutes to closing time. Far from being the happiest place on earth, it instead became a site of bitter resentment and recriminations.

On the fifth day Bird agreed to part with some hard-earned

cash and take Ruby to a nice restaurant. They settled on El Coyote, an affordable Mexican place on Beverly Boulevard, popular with the trendy Hollywood crowd. All was going well, and Bird was chin deep in a plate of carnitas, the mouthwatering shredded pork keeping her mind off her troubles. All of a sudden, she made eye contact with a woman two booths down. She was a photographer Bird had gone out with a few times and diligently avoided ever since. Bird quickly averted her gaze, but then recognized someone else at the bar, a C-list celebrity and bail jumper she had traced a while back for a hit-and-run. His career never recovered from the ensuing bad press, and he'd blamed her for the downfall. Honestly, it was difficult to tell who wished Bird the greater harm, the jilted ex-lover or the disgraced actor, but when both suddenly got up and started walking toward her table Bird decided she wasn't curious enough to find out. She grabbed Ruby's arm and hastily exited. No one in her family knew Bird was gay, and she was not about to come out to her baby sister in the middle of a crowded Mexican restaurant. She had to lie to Ruby about who the strange woman was who'd cursed at them as they left. That, combined with leaving behind food she'd spent good money on, put Bird in the foulest of moods.

On the sixth day Ruby, Bird, and Jesse packed a light lunch and drove around Beverly Hills, that fabled place of ridiculous wealth where money flows through the streets like rivers of Botox. Even the jaded bounty hunter had to admit it was a little exhilarating, seeing all those fancy boutiques on Rodeo Drive, the Jaguars on display at the exotic car dealership on Wilshire, and of course the homes—good Lord, nothing could prepare you for the magnitude of multimillion-dollar homes lined up block after block. So, yes, the drive was fun at first. But slowly, like dusk creeping over what had been a bright, beautiful day, a dark pall fell over them. Both sisters came to the dark realization that no matter how much they worked, regardless of how hard they wished it so, they would probably never be able to shop in those boutiques, they were unlikely to ever get behind the wheel of a Jaguar, and most certain of all, by no stretch of the imagination would either of them ever live in a Beverly Hills mansion. Without having to say a word they recognized the same disappointment on each other's faces—strangely, it was one of the few times they ever agreed on anything. This patch of city and everything it represented were so far out of reach for the Blacker girls that it may as well have been on the moon. They drove in silence back to Bird's tiny apartment, their hearts burdened with bitter insight. Except for Jesse, who happily hummed the theme to *The Beverly Hillbillies* all the way.

On the seventh day Bird rested.

She planned to do absolutely nothing other than run out the clock until she had to take Ruby to the airport for her seven o'clock. flight back to Texas. Then Bird could finally get on with her normal life. She was caught completely off-guard when her mother called around noon with disturbing news: Their aunt, who'd successfully fought off breast cancer five years back, had suffered a relapse, and Bird's mom was on her way to Chicago to help care for her. In the meantime, Ruby would have to remain in L.A. under her older sister's supervision for at least another month.

Bird gritted her teeth so hard she was sure sparks must have shot from her mouth. But there was nothing she could do. It was, after all, a family emergency, and no matter what, family sticks together. Reluctantly, she agreed to look after her little sister.

Unfortunately, this meant there was now another mouth to feed, and Bird was usually low on funds in the best of times. This put her in the awkward position of having to do something very distasteful. She almost would've rather starved, but instead she swallowed her pride and dialed her cell. "Hello, Vicky? Listen, I've changed my mind."

"Who is this?" Da Vinci said nonchalantly.

"You know who this is, you old bag of prunes."

"How charming. It must be Bird Blacker. What can I do for you?"

Bird sighed and continued, "If you still need someone to go after the Veach guy, the tax dodger, I'll do it."

"Sorry, I don't think I'll be needing you after all."

"Oh, my God. You called Mochabean."

"Bird, I had to go with someone else. It's been a week, after all."

"Vicky, please. It's not even about me. I got to take care of my kid sister for another month, and I'm hurting for cash right now."

Vicky remained silent, making Bird squirm for a few painful seconds, then finally said, "All right, but the fee's gone down. I can only give you 9 percent on this one."

"What? You bitch. You concentrated, pasteurized, grade-A bitch!"

"I don't have time for your romance talk. Take it or leave it."

"Fine, whatever," Bird spat.

"Excellent. And Bird?"

"Yeah?"

"I told you you'd be sorry." Then Vicky chuckled.

FORBIDDEN FRUIT AND SERPENTS

BIRD'S APARTMENT WAS BIG enough for a giraffe, but only the crumbly variety that comes in boxes of animal crackers. Still, it was clean—fastidiously so—and it was hers, and she felt most at ease there. Usually.

Dark thoughts roiling within her, Bird paced, ping-ponging back and forth between the posters of Miles Davis on one wall and of Abraham Lincoln on another. This is what every day will be like, she thought. Just when her life was finally settling down. Just when she'd started to even consider dating again, after the recent fiascoes with That Damned Woman and then The Forbidden Fruit. The first was all fire, lust, and baby oil, and though it had been very satisfying sexually, it had ultimately left her feeling empty inside. And the second—well, suffice it to say that if there's a rule indicating "Never Fuck a Coworker," the corollary should state, "That Goes Double for a Coworker's Wife." Past dating snafus aside, Bird was a different woman now. A woman who finally had her shit in order and was moving on with her life. But not with a nosy, impetuous younger sister who needed constant babysitting, she wasn't. Bird felt her life spinning down the drain. Then she heard a flushing sound.

Ruby emerged from the bathroom and made herself comfortable on the well-worn futon. She yawned and stretched comfortably, not a care in the world.

"So, roomie, what are we doing tonight?"

Bird stared at the creature sitting in the middle of her home. The smiling, troublesome creature she'd have to put up with for another month. She'd had enough, felt like a caged tiger, couldn't possibly spend another minute with her. Most of all, she needed a drink. "You can take whatever you want from the fridge. I'll be back later. Lock the door and don't let anyone in."

"Where are you going?"

"None of your business," Bird growled, then slammed the door on the way out.

•

The bar was no more than a fifteen-minute walk from Bird's apartment, and though it welcomed customers of all persuasions, it was normally a homogeneous clientele. Women drank together, played pool together, danced together, and because they kept the bathroom spotless, Bird almost felt at home there. Most of all, it was good to leave behind her family troubles and hang out somewhere she could openly be herself.

Annika, a petite girl in her mid-twenties, sat at the bar drinking a bright-red concoction that matched the color of her short, spiky hair. She frowned, deep in thought, and wrote down an errant bit of code on a napkin. When she noticed Bird sidling up, she welcomed her with a smile. "Bird Blacker, what brings you 'round these parts?"

"I'm looking for a man."

"Sister, are you ever in the wrong place." The elfin girl laughed.

"Beautiful and witty," Bird said sarcastically. "However are you still single?"

"That's what my mom keeps asking." She nudged Bird's side.

"I'm serious, Annika. I need to get this out of the way fast. I got family visiting, and she's making matters complicated."

"You know, I have never heard you say word one about family." Annika drank from her colorful cocktail. "And here I thought you hatched from an egg."

"Don't I wish." Bird signaled the bartender, a Cuban girl with the most perfect, most flawless golden-brown skin she had ever seen. The girl's dazzling smile only accentuated her dark good looks. "Rum and Coke." Maybe someday, Bird thought, as she admired the girl, but not now, not with Ruby here. Grudgingly, she turned away.

"OK, what do I have to work with?" Annika asked.

Bird handed her a slip of paper with Billy Veach's name and identifying information, Social Security and driver's license numbers, and so on. Annika glanced at it, then folded it and put it away.

"Tax dodger. Give me everything you can—credit-card use, checks, anything."

"When do you need it?"

"Yesterday, with a cherry on top."

Annika answered with a raised eyebrow. "I'm a hacker, not a magician."

Yet Annika's abilities were nothing short of supernatural to Bird, who, by comparison, was akin to one of the Neanderthals poking at the obelisk in the movie *2001*. "Do your best," she said, confident that Annika would track down something useful.

"You know, it wouldn't take you that long to learn how to use a computer yourself."

"Then I wouldn't have an excuse to spend time with you, would I?"

Annika caught someone looking their way from across the crowded bar. "Uh-oh, looks like you have a secret admirer," she said with a smirk and nodded to the attractive woman brazenly checking out Bird.

Bird turned and immediately recognized the woman sitting in the booth. She was gorgeous; she raised her drink and motioned Bird over with the confidence of a woman who had never been rejected. That Damned Woman, Bird thought. She looked just as good as Bird remembered, like a shiny, forbidden apple. Actually, though, she was more like the serpent.

"Who's she?" Annika asked, more than a little intrigued.

"Trouble," Bird sighed.

"I could tell that just by looking at her." Annika absentmindedly licked her lips.

"Trust me, whatever she's selling, you don't want it."

"Yeah?" Annika hopped off her stool, ready to go in for the kill. "Maybe she's giving it away today. A nibble couldn't hurt."

Bird stuck her arm out, blocked the redhead's path, and shook her head. She gently pushed Annika back on her stool. "Call me as soon as you find something on Veach. Now, if you'll excuse me, I'd better go see what this can of worms is all about."

Bird walked over to the booth and slid in opposite the woman, who was coolly sipping from her drink. How is it that the second-biggest mistake of her love life wound up in the only place Bird could sit and drink in relative comfort? She considered for a long moment, trying to decide not whether it was a mistake to get involved with this woman again, but rather how big a mistake it would be and how much pain it would lead to this time.

The beauty across from her, never a stranger to admiring stares, finally broke the silence. "Still the strong, silent type, I see."

"Are you following me now?"

"What if I am?" she said playfully. "Haven't you ever been stalked by a jealous ex-girlfriend?"

She couldn't hold back any longer; she had tried, but she was only human. Bird's usually impenetrable shield of stoicism crumbled before the exotic beauty. "You look nice, Kaya," she said, then cracked a grin.

"And you look wound tight as a piano wire. As usual." Kaya reached over to loosen Bird's tie, her hand lingering on the woman's collarbone.

Bird took the hand in hers. She noticed a bandage on the back of it.

"What happened?"

"It's nothing. A stray bit me."

"A dog? What if it had rabies or something?"

"It's not that kind of dog."

Bird frowned, confused. But then Kaya gently squeezed her hand and hit her with a smile so stunning it made the bar and everyone in it disappear from existence. No more banter, no past harms or regrets to complicate matters, only these two women who once upon a time used to wake up tangled in each other's arms.

"Remind me again why we broke up, Bird."

Bird shut her eyes tight before answering, all the bad parts of their intense relationship flooding back. "You're a compulsive liar, completely untrustworthy, and incapable of really loving anyone but yourself."

"Oh, that's right." Kaya pulled away slowly and leaned back in her seat.

What's the matter, sting a little? Can this woman even feel pain? Bird wondered. Because she certainly could inflict it.

After a moment, Kaya continued in that honey voice of hers, "But the sex was good, wasn't it?"

"It's been more than a year since we saw each other last. What are you doing here, Kaya?"

"It hasn't been all that long," Kaya said. "I had a job nearby. So I thought, why not stop by?"

Ah, yes, that mysterious job of hers. The one that had kept her out at all hours of the night, the one that sometimes brought her home with bruises on her face and arms. "You never did tell me what it is you do."

"No, I didn't." Secretive as ever. "How about you, still a cop?"

Bird looked away, recalling a distant pain. "No, I run down bail jumpers now. I decided it was best to move on from the force."

"Oh? I thought you loved that job."

"They didn't appreciate my proclivities, and I didn't appreciate nobody showing up when I called for backup." It had been a little more complicated than that, of course, involving her then partner, his now estranged wife, and Bird's absence of common sense when it came to women she should stay away from. But she was not about to discuss the biggest mistake of her life with the second biggest, now sitting across from her.

"Imagine that, in this day and age. Maybe we can go somewhere quiet, discuss your 'proclivities' in depth." Kaya sipped from her drink slowly, provocatively.

After an excruciatingly long moment, Bird was surprised by the words that came out of her mouth: "I can't. I have family over. They wouldn't . . . understand."

"You haven't told them?" she said, as if it was a new

haircut Bird was keeping from her family, and not her sexual orientation. "And they haven't figured it out?"

"They're from Texas."

"Ah." Kaya nodded. "Well, sure you won't change your mind?"

Bird felt the woman's finger tracing slow circles on her hand. The well-starched bounty hunter licked her suddenly dry lips. Other parts of her were just as suddenly not so dry. Getting together one last time couldn't hurt. Other people had one-nighters all the time. Hell, half the women in the bar would probably end up spending the night at the other half's homes that night. What was wrong with a little stress relief, no strings attached? Lord knows she needed it after the week she'd just been through, never mind the month that lay ahead.

The circles quickened on Bird's hand, as Kaya pressed into the flesh. A devilish smile formed at the corners of her perfect mouth.

And that was the rub, for Kaya did come with strings attached, all sorts of strings. Most of which you didn't even notice until they were already tight around your neck and choking you, so to speak.

"I really can't," Bird finally said. "I got this Billy Veach thing to take care of tomorrow."

Kaya pulled her hand away, folded her arms. "Is this Billy Veach by any chance an accountant?"

"You know him?"

"Unfortunately. He's about as big a loser as you can be without running backward."

"Know where I can find him?" Bird asked hopefully.

"Sorry, can't help you." She was all business now, the honey gone from her voice. "But take my advice and forget about him."

"You sure there's nothing you can give me on him?"

"One thing: he's not worth the trouble."

It didn't take a master detective to realize something was up, but Bird knew better than to push Kaya when she was being reticent. Maybe she could bring it up later, should they . . . run into each other again.

Kaya slid out of the booth, and after a last, lingering look at Bird said, "I'm going now." But before leaving, she leaned over and brushed her lips lightly across Bird's mouth. "Last chance." And she walked away, hips swiveling ever so slightly.

Fuck! Why does trouble always look so damned good? Bird bit her lip in sweet frustration. She was halfway out of the booth, unsure if she should listen to the pesky inner voice screaming at her to Go for It! Listening to that voice usually got her in hot water, but that only reminded her of the time she shared a nice, steamy bath with Kaya.

The final straw was when Kaya walked past Annika at the bar. Seeing an opening, the smaller girl gulped down her drink and swiveled in her chair to chase after the alluring woman. Before her buttocks left the seat, however, Bird was there pushing Annika back onto the stool.

"What's the big idea?" the short redhead complained. "She's fair game."

"I'm doing you a favor," Bird assured her. "You wouldn't want to wake up with rope burns, would you?" Bird then hastily followed her quarry.

Annika pouted. "As a matter of fact, yes, I would."

(5)

REGRETS, I'VE HAD A FEW . . . DOZEN

BIRD WASN'T SURE HOW she ended up at Kaya's place; she wasn't even sure it was Kaya's place, as she'd never seen the apartment before—they had always ended up at Bird's small place when they were seeing each other. All she knew was that Kaya had beckoned and she had followed; it was that simple, that primal. That stupid. What was she thinking getting involved with this woman again? What was she thinking getting involved with any woman while her little sister was in town and could out her to her entire family? She wasn't thinking at all; that was the problem.

Then Kaya's lips were on her mouth. Damn, this woman knows how to kiss, she thought in a fog. There was nothing demure or uncertain about Kaya's hungry kiss; it was pure in its need, undiluted in its desire, fierce, and a little bit intimidating, just like Kaya herself. If Bird didn't know how she got here, she was equally at a loss to explain where her clothes had gone. Somehow she was in only bra and panties, yet still wore her tie. She had on a single shoe, and her long hair, normally pulled back tight, was free and wild and darker than the night around them. As they kissed, Kaya led them toward the bedroom by tugging on Bird's tie, as if leading a leashed pet.

"Where are you taking me?" Bird said coyly.

"What's the matter—don't you trust me?" Kaya tugged harder on the tie, a smile curling her lips.

Bird answered without thinking, "No." Kaya stopped kissing her and released the tie. Bird knew right away she had said something wrong, but it was too late to take it back. Even though women were supposed to be the main proponents of it, she was terrible at this foreplay business, and now her big mouth had ruined the moment. What she should have said was, "Yes, I trust you completely. Now make me see stars, woman." But instead she'd been stupid and answered honestly. Honesty was for fools and martyrs, for people who didn't want to have wild sex involving ropes and chandeliers.

Kaya walked to her bedroom and leaned against the doorway, arms folded. Unlike Bird, who couldn't quite make it out of her clothes, Kaya was completely naked. Even in the darkness her physique was noticeably incredible: firm arms and legs; toned stomach; high, pert breasts; and not an ounce of fat on her. However, it wasn't a gym body, a figure sculpted using weight machines. No, these muscles were earned the old-fashioned way, from actual use. Though she was no bodybuilder, Kaya was powerful; she was proportionately strong, more than a match for anyone, man or woman. "You should always trust your instincts," she said flatly.

Bird tried to read her expression, but there was nothing there to read. The woman was an iceberg, chilly on the surface with only God-knows-what lurking in the depths beneath. The thing about icebergs, they're beautiful to look at, but get too close and they will sink you. So was that it? Was the night over? Feeling frustrated, Bird looked around for the bits of clothing she'd somehow managed to remove during the initial heated moments of their encounter. That settled it: next time she got lucky she wasn't going to utter a single word until the morning after. Or at least until I get all my clothes off, she thought crossly, as she pulled her shirt out from behind the sofa. And I really should put them all in a nice folded pile . . . God! I'm so horny, my teeth hurt!

Then Kaya turned and walked into the dark bedroom. "You coming?" she said over her shoulder.

Bird hesitated only a second. "I was certainly hoping to." She kicked off her shoe and took off her bra, her breasts not quite as pert as Kaya's, but, hey, she'd never gotten any complaints. She almost tripped in the middle of removing her pants, but eventually got them off with an awkward little dance and a lot of hopping about. In the end she still forgot to take off her tie, but no matter—it would come in useful many times during the night.

•

Her watch said it was seven when Bird emerged into the unmistakable Los Angeles morning: It was bright with self-confidence, leisurely in its pace, and just a bit too concerned with itself. Her raven-black hair was back in place, and so was the rest of her outfit, not a wrinkle in sight. Everything was as it should be, except for her tie, which she suddenly realized she was no longer wearing. Where had that gotten to? She didn't feel like going back in to look for it. Things had gotten a bit strange toward the end.

As they were getting dressed, Kaya had asked her, "Ladybird, what do you think about . . . love?"

Bird had felt the sucking pull of the commitment swamp and recoiled instantly, out of pure survival instinct. "Look, last night was great," she had stammered. "Lots of fun, really.

But I'm not looking for anything more than that. Life is too complicated for me as it is."

That had caused Kaya to go cold again. She hardly said another word the rest of the morning. Bird tried to bring her around, even apologized, which she seldom did, but it was no use. Kaya would have none of it; a cool silence was her only response.

Just before walking out the door, Bird had said, "I'm going to be pretty busy for a while, but if you want to talk later . . . " She held the doorknob and waited, one foot already out of the apartment.

Kaya nursed a cup of black coffee in her kitchen. She hadn't replied immediately, instead gazing out the window at the scene below: people on the street went about their daily routines, in groups and alone, couples and families—it was the families her eyes kept drifting toward, the ones with mother and father and child.

When she saw there was no response coming, Bird had turned to leave.

"I'll be seeing you." Kaya had not looked at her when she said it, and Bird detected a strange inflection in her voice, something dark she couldn't quite identify.

Something else strange: their lovemaking had been unusually tender, still ardent, yes, but with none of the hurried aggressiveness Kaya had enjoyed during the many months they had dated, and with few of the obligatory knots and binds. It was almost as if she had been doing her best to start over, to show a new face, to prove that she could be a different person.

Now as she stood outside the apartment, Bird did remember the dark, brick-lined building. It melted into the skyline of Miracle Mile on Wilshire Boulevard, the world-famous museums to the north and the spirit-breaking opulence of

Beverly Hills to the west. She recalled that she had been here
once or twice before, early on when she and Kaya were dating,
and then only to pull up to the curb to pick her up, never to
enter. Last night was different; it was the only time Kaya had
ever let her in.

"Damned batty broads. Just when you think you've figured
them out." She didn't know what to make of Kaya's behavior—
first on fire, then strangely gentle, then frosty. She was still
debating whether to go back for her missing tie—she had
already lost or ruined so much of her wardrobe in the past
week. As she ran her hand down her face in frustration, a slip
of color caught her attention. It was her tie, fastened around
her wrist and tucked into her shirt. She'd been so distracted by
Kaya's moody conduct that she had not noticed it while getting
dressed. Tender she may have been, but Kaya still liked to be in
control when it came to lovemaking.

"Some things never change." She caressed her wrist where
the tie looped around and thought back fondly to the fun they
had had the night before, when there were no bewildering
words or hurt feelings, when it was only arms and legs entwined
and fingers and tongues being put to enthusiastic use, just like
the good Lord intended.

6

MOCHABEAN THE MAN-MOUNTAIN

JESSE DROVE HIS VAN, smiling peacefully as usual, and looked up at the full moon and twinkling stars. It was a gorgeous night, the kind rarely seen inside the city limits. The evening was so beautiful that Jesse began howling in primal appreciation. A hand quickly reached out and gripped his arm.

Bird sulked in the passenger seat. She shook her head, indicating she was in no mood for Jesse's eccentricities. They had spent the past two days looking for any sign of bail-jumper Billy Veach and gotten nothing but a big, fat goose egg. If they didn't pick up his trail soon, chances were he'd be gone for good, maybe even out of the country. That meant no fee for Bird, not even a measly 9 percent. She'd even been forced to bring Ruby along, because she didn't know how long she'd be gone and didn't trust the girl alone in the apartment. Bird rubbed at her forehead with one hand, trying in vain to make a whopper of a headache disappear.

Ruby sat cross-legged in the back of the van, happily digging through a duffel bag full of their equipment.

Bird heard the clattering and turned to her sister. "Be careful with that stuff."

"I just want you to know, it's really cool of you to let me stay an extra month, Ladybird," Ruby said as she examined a pair of shiny handcuffs.

Bird used both hands on her head now and slid down in her seat. Why couldn't I have been an only child? she wondered. "What about your college? Will you miss any classes?"

"Not at all. I dropped out."

Bird turned to Ruby slowly, painfully. "You did what?"

"I'm taking some time off. You know, get to know myself, see what I want to do with my life."

There must be some mistake. People didn't still say things like "get to know myself" in this day and age, in this economy. People finished college—which their older sister happened to be paying for—and they got themselves a job. And they thanked their sister by paying back her kindness at 30 percent interest. "But you will be going back to school?" Bird managed through gritted teeth.

"Maybe. I'm not sure yet."

"And Mom let you? She's fine with this?"

"Oh, yeah, sure. She said I should explore all my options."

"That's funny, because she never let me 'explore my options.'" Bird's left eye twitched, anger bubbling up inside her. "I had to do things like go to summer school—every summer. And you get to drop out. How . . . odd."

"You OK there, Pretty Birdie?" Jesse asked, smirking.

"Just drive," she answered. "And don't ever call me that again." Bird thought about her well-ordered, if not well-to-do, life. A life where she'd come to grips with losing her job as a police officer. A life where she couldn't tell anyone in her family about that particular crushed dream because she hadn't come out to them, and probably wouldn't anytime soon. A life in which she had to live in a tiny apartment, driven by guilt to hand over a large chunk of her salary for her sister's college tuition. And why the guilt? Because she just knew that if her mother ever found out her oldest daughter is a "homosexual," she would promptly drop dead on the spot just to spite Bird. She could see the gravestone now: HERE LIES PETUNIA MARIA BLACKER, FELLED BY HER UNGRATEFUL DAUGHTER, THE LESBIAN. And so Bird paid the money and allayed the guilt. Sure, she lived in an apartment no bigger than a shoe box, but it was her shoe box. Yeah, she tracked down the scum of the earth for a living, but she did it in a professional manner and she got paid. It wasn't a perfect life, but she'd managed to make it work. Then Bird looked at her sister, who, if she were to find out Bird is gay, would tell their mother in a heartbeat. Bird thought about her well-ordered life and imagined it spinning, spinning, spinning till it disappeared down a watery cyclone, followed by a flushing sound. Now both her eyes twitched madly.

"Got something in your eye?" Jesse asked.

"I said shut up and drive," she barked.

"What are you guys exactly?" Ruby tried to put on a Kevlar vest, but she couldn't figure out the straps. "What is all this?" The girl shrugged, then set aside the vest. Instead, she snapped a handcuff onto her wrist and smiled proudly. She looked like a kid in a candy store, which aside from bubble gum and jellybeans also happened to carry ammunition and restraining devices.

"We're bounty hunters, man," Jesse answered.

"We are fugitive-recovery agents," Bird huffed.

"Awesome," said Ruby. "So are we hunting down a murderer, a bank robber?"

"We're not hunting anyone down," Bird said. "I just need to talk to someone who knows a lot of other shady someones."

"Hey, maybe we can be crime-busting partners." Ruby tugged at the handcuff, but it wouldn't come off. She searched in the duffel for a key.

"Not likely," Bird grunted, the sound of her life flushing down the crapper still echoing in her head.

Jesse brought the van to a stop in a quiet suburban neighborhood, in front of a house with a god-awful lawn. Where it wasn't overgrown with waist-high weeds it had patches of dead grass, and broken toys were scattered throughout. Bird jumped out, then quickly turned to her sister and Jesse. "Both of you stay here."

Jesse relaxed in his chair, but not Ruby the human spark plug. "Is this where your snitch lives?" She practically jumped up and down on the van's floor. "Let me come with you, Bird. I can be the good cop; I'll hold you back from ripping out his fingernails with rusty pliers. You guys have rusty pliers, right?"

Bird rolled her eyes, then slammed the door shut in Ruby's eager face. God, was she always this perky? Bird wondered. I can't get through a month of this; I'll go insane.

•

The inside of the house was just shy of squalid, with pizza and Chinese takeout boxes everywhere. Bird sat on a ratty sofa, though she now saw that was a mistake; mystery stains covered the fabric. Truth be told, she wished she could hover three inches off the ground every time she was forced to set foot in this home.

The man who sat across from Bird was dressed like he shopped at a secondhand store with his eyes closed—his clothes were both old and mismatched. But Scoop, as he insisted on being called, was a valuable source of information, with years of experience as a reporter on the police beat. He could usually be counted on for tidbits about who'd done what to whom and where they were hiding out till the heat wore off. Unfortunately, today he seemed preoccupied, staring at Bird with a dazed look.

"Well?" Bird finally said.

"Well what?"

"What have you got on Billy Veach? Why do you think I've been sitting here the last five minutes?"

"Sorry, I haven't been getting much sleep lately," he yawned. "Veach doesn't ring any bells. What'd he go down for?"

"Tax fraud."

"Tax fraud, Veach—let me think." Suddenly, a baseball glove smacked him in the back of the head. Scoop barely flinched; he was used to this kind of abuse. A piercing "Daddy!" could only mean the arrival of his seven-year-old son. The bucktoothed, pudgy boy sported a Little League uniform.

"Daddy, we're going to be late for the game!" the boy screamed.

"In a minute, Sammy. Daddy's earning your college tuition." Scoop ducked as a softball flew past his head.

"Kid's got a good arm," Bird said.

"He's got a temper on him is what he's got." Scoop patted the back of his head where the glove had hit him. "You know kids—no patience."

•

Back in the van, Ruby pouted in the passenger seat, arms folded, glaring straight ahead. "I'll never get to kick ass at this rate. I should be in there with the pliers."

Jesse's legs stretched across the dashboard. "That wouldn't work anyway. Violence only begets violence."

"What are you, Yoda?" Ruby sneered.

Jesse did his best impersonation of the diminutive Jedi: "Yoda I am not. Way of yoga do I follow."

But the effort was lost on Ruby, who stared at him blankly.

"I practice 'ahimsa'—nonviolence. It's one of the five re-straints of classical yoga."

"Are you jerking me?" she asked suspiciously.

"No, jerk, yoga is a great lifestyle."

"But then, how can you be a bounty hunter? You being a— what do you call it—a yogurt?"

"I'm a yogi."

"Like the bear? Cute." The girl smiled, no doubt picturing Jesse scampering about looking for pic-a-nic baskets. "So, how did you end up with Bird?"

"I was actually your sister's first."

Ruby's smile suddenly drooped. "Never mind. I don't need to know."

"No, man, nothing pervy. I was the first skip your sister tracked when she became a bounty hunter." He readjusted his position in the chair, kicked his legs farther out on the dashboard to get more comfortable, and closed his eyes.

"So, you're a . . . " Ruby whispered the word, "'criminal'?"

Jesse opened one eye, peeked at the girl. "'Criminal'? No, it was a simple misunderstanding regarding some hallucinogenic 'medication.' Turns out you need a prescription for everything these days. Which just goes to show the abusive power of the medical-industrial complex."

"Are you anywhere near the point?" Ruby yawned. "Because you're losing me fast."

"Fine." He threw both arms behind his head. "Bird busted me at the Burger Hut where I worked. They fired me. So I tracked her down."

"Ah, for revenge," Ruby said knowingly.

"No, for a job." He mimicked angry movements. "I was all, 'You got me fired, lady. You owe me a job.' And she was like, 'Screw off, hippie.' Basically, I nagged her to hire me as her assistant."

"And she hired you?"

"Oh, she didn't want to. She said, 'Why would I hire you? What do you know about being a bounty hunter?' So I look her dead in the eye, and I tell her, 'I tracked you down, didn't I?'"

"Ah-ha, how ironic! She had no choice but to hire you then."

"Actually, she punched me in the gut and called me a 'filthy stalker.'" Jesse patted his stomach at the memory. "She only gave in when her car broke down and I offered the use of my van."

"That sounds like Ladybird, all right."

"Yeah, we've been together ever after."

Just then, the van shuddered violently. Both Ruby and Jesse were thrown about like rag dolls amid the terrible sound of crunching metal. They picked themselves up quickly and looked around confused.

"What happened?" Ruby asked. "Was that an earthquake?"

In the rearview mirror Jesse saw headlights behind them. "Someone hit my van, man!"

"Well, come on then, scruffy, let's get out there and kick some ass," she said eagerly.

Ruby leaped into the night air first, fists clenched and ready for action despite the single handcuff that still dangled from her wrist. Jesse, on the other hand, tumbled out of the vehicle, not quite ready for solid ground. He was horrified to find a pickup where none should be: pushed grill-deep into his van's rear bumper.

"Hey, butt face, who taught you to drive?" Ruby strode defiantly up to the truck.

The pickup door opened, and a giant emerged.

He was six-foot-seven, bald, with muscles on his muscles, and a scowl you couldn't scrape off with a chisel. The man-mountain did not look happy, and the cold brunt of his anger was aimed squarely at Jesse.

"Oh, shit." Jesse's knees almost buckled under him. "It's Mochabean."

•

In the house, Scoop the informant peered into Bird's eyes, almost like he was trying to look into her soul, or at least past her corneas. "You ever plan on having kids?" he asked.

"Do I look like the motherly sort?" She frowned. "Besides, I don't lead the right lifestyle."

"Oh, you mean 'cause you're . . . " He broke eye contact, seemed embarrassed.

"I'm what?"

"You know." He squirmed in his seat.

"No, please, tell me what I am." Bird leaned forward, challenging him.

"You know . . . a lesbian. Jeez, that's all. Is that wrong now? All of a sudden we can't call people lesbians anymore?"

"No, you dope, I can't have kids because I could get my head shot off at any given moment. Plenty of dykes have kids."

"Oh, sure, they do like horse breeders, with that artificial insemi—"

"Scoop!" she cut him off, dragging a hand down her face in frustration. "Can we get back to the Veach matter?"

"Oh, right. Let me think."

Scoop's kid screamed out of nowhere, "D-a-a-a-ddy!" He pitched a baseball bat straight at his father's head. The solid wood flew fast and true, and Scoop was not going to dodge this one. It looked like the evening would include a trip to the emergency room, when Bird snagged the bat in midair, inches from the man's face.

"The joys of parenthood," he said, breathing hard. "See what you're missing out on?"

"Duly noted." Bird turned to the boy, who flashed a toothy smile. That's not a child, she thought, that's a barracuda with legs. No way am I ever having kids. Not that she had ever seriously considered having children of her own, at least not without a half bottle of vodka in her, a deep feeling of soul-crushing loneliness creeping over her as she sat alone in her minuscule apartment staring at the ceiling at three in the morning. But that's normal, right? Everyone felt like that—gay or straight— like they're going to die alone, unloved, and insignificant. Like the only possible way to lift that overwhelming darkness, to feel like your existence mattered to some small degree, was the sound of tiny feet running to you when you got home, the feel of a fat, little hand gripping yours for support, the sight of two big, innocent eyes looking to you for guidance . . . Well, maybe someday . . . Bird sighed. I have enough people to take care of for now.

•

Jesse stood frozen with fear, unable to run back into the van, and certainly unwilling to keep going forward into the grasp of the furious giant. It was all he could do to keep his legs steady. He'd seen what Mochabean could do to a human being; it wasn't pretty, and it wasn't something he wanted to experience himself.

"Joey Dunlap was my skip!" the bald Goliath bellowed. "You

guys stole him from under me! You don't take another man's bounty—that's basic rules. You owe me two grand."

"You owe us, ugly," Ruby said, face-to-stomach with Mochabean. "Look what you did to our van."

But the towering Mochabean ignored little Ruby; she didn't even register on his radar. His gaze remained laserlike on the now hyperventilating Jesse. "Where is she? Where's Bird?"

Ruby moved right under Mochabean and jumped up and down to get his attention. "Hey, I'm talking to you. You better have insurance."

"Ruby," Jesse whispered, "come back here, please." He waved his arm frantically.

Ruby looked at the faltering Jesse, then at the huge Mochabean, then back at Jesse. "What? You're scared of this guy?" She pointed with her thumb at the monster.

"Hey, uh, Mochabean." Jesse's voice cracked with fear. He cleared his throat and soldiered on. "Haven't seen you at the Banana Cabana lately, man. I look around the bar, and I think, where's my big, bald buddy?"

Mochabean glared, his words crawling out like meat from a grinder. "I. Want. My. Money." He took a step toward Jesse. "Where's Bird?"

"Bird ain't here right now, man." Jesse stepped back. "But we'll let her know you wanna chat, OK?"

"Fine. I'll take it out of your hide." Mochabean lunged toward Jesse, unusually fast for such a large creature. Ruby, little more than a speed bump, got knocked aside. Her head hit the sidewalk, making her woozy and temporarily knocking her out of action.

"Holy . . . " is all Jesse had time for as Mochabean swung a meaty fist at his head. Small and nimble, he ducked out of the way, but he wasn't quite fast enough. Mochabean snagged him by the shirt collar. The big man yanked up Jesse and pinned him against the side of the van, then choked the breath from him.

"If I don't get my money, you don't get to breathe," Mochabean said.

Jesse gasped for air, pulled and yanked at Mochabean's thick arms, but he didn't even budge them. The hands, like two slabs of granite, tightened around his neck. Jesse's eyes rolled back in their sockets.

•

"Come on, Scoop, switch on a synapse, will ya?" Bird said.

"Wait, wait, the name Veach does sound familiar." The disheveled man put a finger to his head. "No, never mind. I'm thinking of a commercial I saw on TV for jumping balloons. Some party place rents 'em out. Made my kid go nuts. Now he wants one for his birthday."

"Jesus," Bird muttered and rolled her eyes. Then she noticed a mysterious lump on the carpet—no, it was actually under the carpet. And had it just moved? She poked at it with the baseball bat and scrunched her nose in disgust. How can a human being live like this? she wondered. Even growing up, Bird's room was unlike any teenager's: clothes folded, no trace of clutter, and bed always made. But for some reason, obsessive-compulsive cleanliness never earned her any points with the cool kids in school. A loud banging noise broke her reverie. "What is that?"

•

The van's headlights flickered every time Mochabean whomped Jesse against the side of the vehicle. The smaller man's legs dangled uselessly in the air, and his oxygen-deprived face had picked a lovely shade of blue for the evening. Still, he had just enough life in him to gasp out, "I know . . . I know . . . "

"You know where my money is?" Mochabean loosened his grip slightly, enough for Jesse to suck in some breath.

"I know why you hurt, man," Jesse said.

What?" said Mochabean, understandably confused.

"I've seen you sitting all alone at the Banana Cabana. I see the pain in your eyes."

"What the hell you talking about, hair ball?" He squinted at Jesse.

"I can help you, but you gotta let me in, man. You gotta let down your defenses. Let me in."

Mochabean looked around, unsure what to make of Jesse's pleas to "let him in." Usually, the people he dealt with whined and begged for him to "Let me out!" Sometimes they requested that he "Stop, Jesus, you're breaking my arm!" and, of course, there was plenty of "Ahh, ahh, it hurts!" Mochabean knew exactly how to deal with all those situations: apply fist to whiner's jaw, stomach, or crotch, whichever was more convenient. But this "I can help" business—it was just plain perplexing.

•

Bird found herself equally perplexed in Scoop's home, where the slouch had just grabbed a box of Chinese takeout—a box that was a week old at least—from a tabletop and was poking around in it with a fork. No, he couldn't possibly be about to— oh, good Lord, he was eating out of the grimy container! Bird pushed down the waves of nausea rising from her stomach.

Unaware the effect his eating habits were having on his guest, Scoop slurped a noodle as he talked. "Billy Veach. I know a Bil-

ly Bang. He's wanted for unlawful congress with animals . . . "
He sucked the long noodle from the stained box.

It was all Bird could do to keep from knocking the box out
of his hand. How long is that vile thing? she wondered, just
as the tail end slithered out, spun around and around, then
disappeared into Scoop's mouth. And this man is a parent?

"Wait, I've got it!" he declared, sending a tendril flying splat
against Bird's cheek.

"Oh, my God! Oh, my sweet Lord!" She pulled out a neatly
folded handkerchief and wiped frantically at her face.

•

Mochabean furrowed his brow in confusion. "You . . . you don't
know what the hell you're talking about," he told Jesse.

"Let people in, and they'll do the same for you," Jesse assured
him. "You don't have to be alone, man."

"I—I don't." Mochabean's frown eased a bit, his state of
mind shifting from I'll-Kill-You to I'll-Listen-to-You-Then-
I'll-Kill-You.

"Man, but you gotta stop pushing people away." Jesse talked
in soothing tones, much as he had with the monster dog that
mistook Bird for a chew toy. "Remember, violence just creates
barriers to authentic communication."

And much like the canine, Mochabean seemed to respond
positively to the sound of Jesse's words. He lowered Jesse to
the ground. The giant contemplated Jesse's smiling face, not
entirely comfortable with leaving an opponent in one piece.
Truly, this was a bold new direction for Mochabean.

Suddenly, a ragged war cry tore through the night air. Ruby
jumped onto Mochabean's back and pounded away at his bald,
baffled head. "Leave him alone!" she screamed in his ear.

"Ruby, no," Jesse called.

Mochabean, back on comfortable ground, grabbed his assailant and threw her off with minimum effort. She was nothing to him, a flea. "Get lost, small-fry."

With surprising agility, Ruby hit the ground rolling and was back on her feet, ready for more.

"You almost had me going there," Mochabean sneered at Jesse. "All that peace and love jib-jab." With one large paw, he pinned Jesse against the van like a bug in a display case, then swung back his other arm to finish him off.

But Ruby leaped at his arm and clicked a handcuff on his wrist, preventing the deathblow and linking her to Mochabean. He turned and saw Ruby hanging off his arm; she was so small that her feet swung off the ground.

"Try and shake me now, gruesome." She grinned.

"Who are you supposed to be?"

"Ruby Blacker, professional badass." With her free hand she punched him square in the face. The strike would have broken a normal man's nose, yet it was hardly enough to make Mochabean blink.

He dropped Jesse to deal with this new inconvenience. "You're through, kid."

Only then did it occur to Ruby that she had no keys to open the cuffs. She was trapped. "Uh-oh." She pulled in vain at the stainless-steel links as Mochabean turned to her, familiar scowl back in place. He popped his knuckles menacingly, and his bulging arm muscles seemed even larger than before, easily capable of breaking Ruby in half.

"Mochabean!" a woman's voice called out from behind.

"What?" he turned, annoyed.

A baseball bat cracked against the big man's skull, violently snapping his head to the side. Mochabean ever so slowly craned his head back and saw Bird standing before him, bat in hand. He grunted at her, "Huh, you're gonna have to do better than—"

Crack, crack, crack!—Bird bashed his head with three more swift strikes of the bat. Go down, you son of a bitch . . . Please, please, pl-e-e-ease, go down, she thought and held what was left of the splintered bat high. Her breathing came hard and ragged as she watched the immense bounty hunter waver on his legs. Then he dropped like a chopped redwood.

Thank you, baby Jesus. Bird sighed with relief and took a moment to straighten out her disheveled clothes and hair. She handed what was left of the shattered bat to Scoop's boy, who stood nearby with his father. Both looked on with mouths agape. "Sorry about your bat," Bird told the boy.

But he was far from displeased. In fact, he seemed amazed as he looked from Mochabean crumpled on the street to the jagged bat in his little hands. "Sweet!" the boy exclaimed.

So now Bird Blacker had contributed to the further corruption of America's young minds. Oh, well, it was no worse than what you saw in your average hooker-bashing, car-stealing video game these days.

Mochabean had it coming. Sure, technically she did steal one of his skips right out from under him while he was changing a flat on his truck. And, yeah, in principle you weren't supposed to steal another man's skip—part of the bounty hunter's unwritten code of honor. But, hell, Bird had been at a low point in her life, having just lost her police job and with bill collectors hounding her like wolves (wolves with a recently acquired taste for the flesh of credit-card debtors). It hadn't been her proudest moment—nor even the worst, for that matter—but you held your nose and did what you must to get along in this town. Besides, nobody picked on Bird Blacker's little sister.

"Should I call the cops?" Scoop offered.

"It's better if we just leave," Bird said. She helped Jesse stand, even as he tried to reacquaint himself with the art of breathing. "Come on, time to scram."

"Violence . . . not the answer," he wheezed. "God, my windpipe."

"You know better than to mess with Mochabean," she scolded. "What got into you?"

As if on cue, Ruby grunted from under Mochabean, whose thick arm had pinned her down. "A little help here?" She jiggled her handcuffed hand. "Anybody got the keys?"

7

STARCH AND DESTROY

BY EIGHT THIRTY IN the morning, Bird began ironing every item of clothing she owned. She tried to work quietly in the living room, the only place the ironing board fitted in the apartment, so as not to disturb her sleeping sister. She need not have worried; Ruby still snored deeply, sprawled out on the futon in the middle of Bird's apartment. She'd been there only a little more than a week, and already the usually immaculate home looked noticeably worse for wear—magazines spread all over the coffee table, a shoe sticking out of a bookshelf, the TV remote jammed under Ruby's face as she drooled on it. Bird cringed at the sight. Must remember to disinfect that.

An hour later, Bird was ironing her favorite pair of pants. She sprayed starch on them for a good eight seconds before sliding the superhot metal over the fabric. "Almost there." She sprayed another absurdly long burst, then ironed a perfect crease down the middle of the leg. She looked over her work, then sprayed once more. Bird smiled contentedly, like a kid who'd gotten to stay up late on a school night.

Ruby slowly opened a drowsy eye. "Isn't that Mom's old ironing board?"

"Good, you're up. Yes, she let me have it when I moved."

"Why are you ironing this early in the morning?" She yawned, stretched, then found a comfortable new position on the futon.

"It's not that early. Besides, if you take care of your clothes, they'll take care of you."

"Funny, that's what Mom always says." She rubbed at sleep-filled eyes.

Bird reflexively winced at being compared to her mother. They were nothing alike, as anyone who knew them could plainly see. Her mother was judgmental, strict, close-minded, a nag. And Bird was, well, not any of those things, she was certain. She examined her troublesome little sister, all limbs and angles on the futon. "Have fun last night?"

Ruby's eyes popped wide, the slumber burned away by memories of the fight with Mochabean. "Did you see the way that guy went down?" she said, beaming. "I was whaling away pretty good on him before you got there." She mimicked her mighty blows raining down on a hapless Mochabean.

"You're going back home tomorrow," Bird said matter-of-factly.

Ruby jumped to her feet. "No! Why?"

"I can't have you getting in the way." Though her voice remained calm, Bird pressed the iron hard on the pants. She knew she was in for a fight and hunkered down mentally for the struggle. The line of her mouth got thinner and tighter with each stroke of the iron.

"I won't get in the way," Ruby whined. "I'll just tag along and take notes."

"Like you did last night? What were you thinking?" She pounded the iron, taking out her anger on the defenseless pants.

"I had to do something."

"What, get killed so he gets more prison time? Don't you ever think before you jump into things?" Steam hissed from the iron, as if it too was thoroughly displeased with Ruby's headstrong ways.

"I could've taken him . . ." Ruby slumped back onto the futon. "I could have!" Dejected, the girl reached for a poster of Lincoln that was hanging just above her on the wall. Lincoln was a hero of Bird's—the only hero she could ever recall having, in fact—a brilliant, courageous man who paid with his life for doing the right thing. And he declared Thanksgiving a national holiday, so, thanks for that too, Abe.

"Don't touch that," Bird commanded, the calm in her voice quickly dissipating.

"You know, your place is kinda small."

"It's what I can afford." A final blast emptied out the can of starch. Bird shook it, then clanged the useless can on the coffee table. "Who do you think's been paying for your tuition?"

"Hey, I never asked you to."

"No, that was Mom. 'Ladybird, it's your duty to help out the family,'" she mimicked her mother and wagged a finger. "So now I live in this box and ride around in Jesse's crapmobile . . ." Her exterior calm shattered completely. Bird slammed the iron on the board, pressed, and twisted down. "And now you decide to 'find yourself,' so I lose the twenty grand I've paid in tuition." She walked over to Ruby and stared her down.

The girl squirmed uncomfortably under her sister's glare. To break the tension she swiped a magazine from the coffee table and pretended to read. She held the magazine high to hide her face. "I didn't think I was such a burden . . ."

"That's the problem. You never think. You just do as you please and let the rest of us clean up after you." She was a little embarrassed to find she had both hands on her hips, in the traditional Disapproving Mom pose. The same pose she'd seen her own nagging mother use many a time against her. The pose Bird swore she would never use. She quickly slid her hands in her pockets, hoping she looked more like a hip older sister (which she totally was) than an old-fashioned matron (which she wasn't. At all. Really.).

"God, what crawled up your butt?" Ruby flung the magazine across the table, where it pushed several other glossies over the edge.

Bird frowned, picked up the strays, and rearranged the magazines into a perfect pile. She adjusted the pile to sit exactly in the center of the table. That way you could reach for a magazine with equal ease from any side. She did this because, well, because Ruby certainly would never think to be so considerate. And besides, she couldn't have *Cosmo, Newsweek,* and *Psychology Today* covering her floor like it was a goddamned birdcage! She may have to put up with a small apartment, but she hadn't yet been reduced to living in squalor! And now what was making that scraping noise, for fuck's sake? She looked around for the sound's origin, then realized it was her, grinding her teeth in frustration.

"We gonna hunt down some bad guys now, or what?"

"All we're hunting is the cheapest airfare back to Texas," Bird said sternly and took out her cell phone. "You can stay on your own for a month, till Mom gets back."

"Bird, you can't!"

"Watch me."

Moving quick as a rabbit, Ruby jumped to her feet and kicked the phone out of Bird's hand. It landed with a thud on the carpet.

"Damn it, what are you . . . ?" Bird eyed her sister suspiciously. She reached down, picked up the phone, and dialed again.

Ruby lashed out with her right leg and kicked the phone into the air, then she followed through with a spin kick in midair that sent the phone flying across the room. Her movements were smooth, practiced, and executed in less than a second. She moved her body with complete self-confidence; her face, however, betrayed her worry.

"How . . . ? What . . . ? How . . . ?" Bird found it difficult to continue, her mouth wide with shock. She pointed at the cell phone, then back at Ruby accusingly. "What's going on here? How did you do that?"

"I'm a black belt." Ruby grinned. She puffed out her chest proudly and stood a little straighter.

"Since when?"

"I've been in tae kwon do for years."

"A black belt. You?" Bird could remember beating up at least a dozen boys in middle school for picking on her little sister, and now she was a black belt? She moved so fast she was a blur when she kicked things. Kicked things in midair! This made no sense.

"I can take care of myself. You'd know if you ever called home." Ruby suddenly tensed. Then she leaped at her big sister, the former school-yard champion.

Still shaky, Bird recoiled and held up her hands protectively. "Don't you dare hit me!" Imagine, getting beaten up by your own baby sister. What sort of bounty hunter would she be then?

But Ruby wasn't attacking. Instead, she ran past, flew over the coffee table, and snatched the iron from the now scorched slacks. In all the commotion, Bird had forgotten she left the iron facedown.

"Damn it, my pants!" Bird wailed. They now featured a large, black mark on the left buttock, as if she'd been branded, like the livestock of a rancher fond of geometric shapes. She glared at Ruby in accusation.

Before Bird could figure out how to blame her for this

latest misfortune, they heard the familiar bleating of Jesse's van outside.

Saved by the horn, Ruby exclaimed, "To the crapmobile!" and made her escape. Bird knew fuming would do little good now. Still, it had served her well in the past, and she excelled at it. So fume she did as she looked for another pair of pants to wear.

•

Bird sat on the van's passenger side and talked on her cell phone. She took notes in a small black notebook. Her handwriting, like the notebook itself, was minute and efficient. "Come on, Annika, give me something," she pleaded into the phone. "You're my last hope. He must have used a credit card, an ATM . . . A gym? What gym? Okay, I guess it's better than nothing. Thanks, doll." She hung up and continued writing.

Jesse slumped in his seat as he drove. He looked over at his partner, but she ignored him. He inhaled deeply to get her attention. When that didn't do the trick, he sucked in even more air. "Ow!" he howled in pain, then poked at his rib cage and grimaced.

Bird sighed and turned finally. "What?"

"You shouldn't take deep breaths when you're slouched over. Your ribs dig into your lungs, man." He pointed at Bird's writing. "Make a note of it."

Without missing a beat, Bird wrote in her notebook and said, "'Jesse is an idiot.' Got it. Anything else?"

"Such negative karma." He shook his head in disappointment. "So, what's the plan?" He craned his neck to sneak a peek at her notes, but she slammed the book shut.

"Head to Big Ape's Gym on Alvarado Street. Annika says

someone's been using this guy's membership for the past week."

Suddenly, a flash from the back of the van blinded them. Bird turned and found her little sister grinning as she held a Polaroid camera aimed at them. A picture whirred out from underneath, and Ruby yanked it out and fluttered it around like a spasmodic butterfly.

"What's that for?" Bird asked, only slightly annoyed.

"To take pictures of evidence," Ruby said.

"What evidence?"

"You know, at the crime scene. Like they do on *CSI*."

Bird and Jesse exchanged a look that said, Is she kidding? When it was evident she wasn't, Jesse piped in, "Uh, dude, that's not what we do."

"It's not?"

Bird couldn't have hidden her smirk if she had tried. And she certainly wasn't about to try. "We don't solve crimes, Columbo. We retrieve fugitives. Fugitive-recovery agents, remember? No *CSI*, no clues, no need for a camera."

"Oh." Ruby looked like someone had just popped her favorite balloon.

Bird should have felt proud that she had finally shut her sister's incessant yaphole—the girl had it coming, after all. Yet, strangely, she felt guilty at seeing Ruby's downcast face. This is all because of the Oldest-Sibling Guilt Complex that Mom burned into my psyche, Bird thought. No matter how far away I move, that woman is always screwing with my head. Bird turned away from the problems of her past and faced forward in her chair, toward the all-new problems that eagerly awaited ahead. Just twenty-nine days, that's all she had left to endure, then Ruby would be gone and she could get back to her normal life—*normal* being a relative term, when just the previous week she'd barely escaped Death by Dog Overdose.

Ruby reached over, hugged Bird, and flashed a picture of them together. Despite herself, Bird looked down at the blank Polaroid. The first image to develop was Ruby's megawatt smile, then the rest of her perky self, and finally her arm around a frowning, dour Bird. Great, even the Instamatic developing process played favorites.

Ruby shoved the picture at an angle into a nook on the van's dashboard. "Maybe it'll come in useful later."

Bird feigned disinterest, but could see the picture out of the corner of her eye. When Ruby returned to the rear of the van, Bird reached down and casually straightened the photo.

"So what's this Veach guy look like?" Ruby sat Indian style, with perfect posture, yet not at all stiff. She always looked so at ease.

Bird shot her a stern look in response. That's all she needed, Ruby trying to "help" her chase down a skip. Just like she'd "helped" with Mochabean.

"What? Looking at a picture won't kill me."

In fact, if there was any way for a picture to endanger her life, and therefore complicate Bird's, Ruby would probably discover it. Reluctantly, she handed her eager sister a picture of the skip, Billy Veach, currently on the lam for cheating on his taxes.

"How long does it usually take to catch a bail jumper? A couple of hours?" Ruby squinted at the picture of Veach, attempting to memorize every nuance of the criminal's features. But he didn't really look like a criminal—no jagged scar across his face, no prison tattoos, no menacing glare. In his late twenties, he was already balding and slightly pudgy, and he had dark circles under his eyes. He looked exactly like what he was: an overworked accountant.

"A couple of hours?" Bird scoffed. "That only happens on TV shows. On your *CSI*."

"Maybe we'll get lucky," Ruby said. Just then, something right outside the van window caught her eye. She looked down at the picture in her hand and wrinkled her brow in concentration. Then she looked back out the window and smiled.

"Tracking down someone takes carefully honed, razor-sharp skills. Skills you don't get from watching cop shows where everyone looks like a damned fashion model. I mean, seriously, have you seen what they wear? Tailored suits, name-brand shoes." Bird looked down in disgust at her off-the-rack outfit. "And the hairstyles! They must spend hours on that alone. What real cop has the time and money to—"

"Oh, my God, there he is!" Ruby squealed as she pointed out the window.

A long, black Lincoln Town Car pulled up next to the van. Not in itself newsworthy, except for the nervous, disheveled mess riding in the backseat of the luxury vehicle—Billy Veach in the pasty flesh. His eyes darted back and forth as he absorbed his surroundings. When he looked up into the morning sky, he resembled a frightened field mouse that's just heard the piercing cry of a hawk circling overhead.

"Son of a . . . ," Bird said in disbelief. She snagged the picture back from Ruby and compared it to the man in the Lincoln. "It is him!"

Veach was probably going to his gym; they were headed that way themselves to look for him. Ruby just happened to look out as his car drove alongside. Pure dumb luck, that's all it had been. If anything, it was Bird's legwork and contacts that had placed them in the perfect spot to locate him. But of course now Ruby would get all the credit.

"Nice pointing skills, Ruby," Jesse joked.

"It's all in the wrist." She flicked her hand, pointing right at the bail jumper it had taken her all of thirty seconds to find.

"But how did you get them so razor sharp?" Jesse continued.

"Shut up and follow that car," Bird grumbled.

•

Billy Veach's driver grinned menacingly into the rearview mirror. Billy shuddered slightly as he met her gaze. He rubbed his arms, pretending he was cold, though he was actually scared to death of the assassin.

"You should listen to your dad and leave the country, Billy," she said from the front seat. "He only wants what's best for you."

"What he wants is me as far away from the cops as possible. Especially since I handle his books."

"Smart boy. You are your father's son." She fixed her gaze on him. "You're lucky, you are." For a split second there was cold fire in her eyes.

He had to prove he was no pushover. "Just what do you mean by that?" he asked, in what no doubt was meant to be a challenging tone but instead exited his mouth as a croak.

"Getting arrested for tax fraud. That was sloppy. You've put Mr. V's entire operation at risk. Especially now that he's under investigation. If you weren't family, I would've handled this . . . differently."

"Are you threatening me?" The only response he got was a subzero smile in the rearview mirror. He huddled into a corner of the large backseat, this time genuinely feeling chilled to the bone.

•

"Don't get so close. They'll see us." Bird hovered by Jesse as he drove. It took all her willpower to keep from grabbing the steering wheel herself.

"Back off, man. I'm a professional." Jesse pushed her face away.

Meanwhile, Ruby nearly vibrated with excitement. "I can't believe we're actually tailing someone. This is too cool." She raised a hand to high-five her sister.

Bird ignored the gesture, though Ruby's grimy hand did remind her it had been hours since she had last washed her own hands. From her pocket, she pulled out a small bottle and squirted a clear glob on each hand, then rubbed them vigorously.

"What's that?" Ruby asked.

"Nothing," Bird said.

Jesse looked over and snorted. "It's hand disinfectant. She always carries it with her. Weird, huh?"

"It is not weird. We deal with people of . . . questionable hygiene." Bird folded her arms defensively.

"You're just like Mom," Ruby said, shaking her head. "She always carries a bottle of Plumeria soap with her too."

Bird thought she could let it go. She thought her willpower was strong enough to keep her from even dignifying that patently absurd statement with an answer. She thought if she folded her arms tighter against her chest, it would keep the words down in her gut. She thought wrong.

Bird spun to face Ruby. "Plumeria soap? Plumeria? That's some crap from Bath & Body Works that smells like fresh-cut daisies and newborn kittens. It packs no punch. This," she held up her bottle, "is an industrial-strength isopropanol-based gel ten times more effective than any fruity-tooty stuff Mom carries. This will kill 99.99 percent of all known microorganisms, and probably some we don't know about yet. All Mom cares about is that stuff smells ladylike and purty. This is nothing you will ever see Mom carrying, do you hear me? Nothing. I've never even set foot in Bath & Body Works." Her chest heaved, and she gripped the bottle so tight that her hand was chalk white. A single bead of sweat trickled down her brow.

Confused and shocked, Ruby turned to Jesse for a possible explanation of why Bird hated Bath & Body Works with such ferocity. All he could offer was a shrug.

"The gym's up ahead," Bird said. And that was that.

8

THE IMPORTANCE OF FACE RECOGNITION

ASIDE FROM BEING A prominent figure in the Los Angeles criminal underground, Mr. V was exceptionally health conscious—some would even call him a health freak, though not to his face, obviously. Even when he wasn't exercising at the gym, he was constantly in motion, jogging in place, stretching, tapping his foot, anything to burn calories. He hadn't always been so active; in his younger years he'd loved rich Italian food and plenty of it, followed by dessert, followed by a nice, long nap. Then his heart decided enough was enough and promptly quit pumping on his fifty-fifth birthday.

His cardiologist pleaded with him to change his lifestyle, but Mr. V was a proud and stubborn man, unwilling to accept that there was anything wrong with the way he chose to live his life. He'd informed the doctor, "Look, just fix my ticker. That's what you do, right? So do your job." It took another two heart attacks in the next two years to finally convince the crime boss that it wouldn't kill him to have a salad every now and again, whereas his regular diet had already attempted to kill him three times.

Sweat poured down Mr. V's face as he peddled on a stationary bike at his favorite gym, Big Ape's on Alvarado. He was a regular at the place, yet nobody ever tried to befriend him or make small talk—due, perhaps, to the fact that there were always two large gentlemen at his side. They did their best to blend in by dressing in black tracksuits, but the gun-shaped bulges in the suits gave them away every time.

The gangster slowed when his cell phone rang, but he didn't stop peddling. "You got him?"

"He's right here, sir," the assassin answered, still driving the Lincoln. "We're five minutes away."

"Excellent. Bring him to me. And one more thing . . . "

"Sir?"

"Play nice. He is family."

She flashed her passenger another subzero smile. "I wouldn't touch a hair on him, sir."

A forlorn Billy Veach sat in the back of the Lincoln and didn't even try to hide his discomfort at her icy smile.

When they reached the gym parking lot, Billy made sure to let the driver get at least ten paces ahead of him as she walked toward the main entrance. He was that spooked of the woman in the dark tailored suit.

•

Jesse slowly pulled the van into the gym parking lot. Ahead, they could see Billy Veach, their target. He was shuffling along, dragging his feet, and seemed completely unaware that he'd been followed.

"This is it." Bird hoped her voice conveyed authority, calm, and no misgivings whatsoever about having her little sister along. "Be ready to get us out fast."

"You just give the word, man, and I am lightning itself." Jesse twisted his hands on the steering wheel.

"Wait for it . . . Wait for it . . . "

Ruby jumped up and down in her seat. "Oh, God, I can't take the suspense. Do it already. Let's nab this sucker."

"Wait for it . . . Now! Gun it!"

The van lunged forward. It screeched to a stop in front of a very startled Billy Veach. When the side door slid open, he was too stunned to react. Bird reached out, grabbed Billy, and yanked him into the van in less than two seconds.

"Go!" she commanded Jesse, as she cuffed Billy. "Drive it like you stole it!"

Jesse hammered the gas pedal, and for the first time in its twenty-five-year existence, the van made a passable impersonation of a dependable vehicle, instead of the jalopy it really was. They cleared the lot in seconds, before the assassin had a chance to interfere. By the time she gave chase, the van was already on the street.

In the rearview mirror, Jesse could see a very pissed-off woman in a very nice suit running after them. "Suck on my dirt, loser!" he cried out.

The enforcer ran till she could run no more, then she pulled out her gun. She tried to get a bead on them, but the van sped around a corner and out of her sights. However, she did catch a glimpse of one of the passengers: Ladybird Blacker. Her mouth formed a smile, but the expression was hollow, bereft of any joy whatsoever. "Unbelievable. Life just got more complicated."

In the back of the van, Billy lay facedown, hands handcuffed behind him. Bird kept a knee at his back to prevent any sudden movements. All things considered, this had turned out a lot easier than she'd dared to hope. "Just like clockwork," she said, a dash of disbelief coloring her voice. "That's how smooth every job should be."

Billy twisted around enough to get a look at his captors. "Who are you people? Don't kill me . . . "

"Nobody's gonna kill you, man." Jesse smiled down at the bail jumper. "We're the good guys." To reassure him that this was so, he gave Billy a thumbs-up. Bad guys would never have bothered with such a gesture.

"Good guys?" Billy asked, puzzled.

Ruby was almost beside herself with glee now. She was a famine victim at an all-you-can-eat buffet, finally getting all the big-city action she craved. "What now, Bird? Do we send him up the river? Or the big house? Or the joint? Is there a difference?"

"I want to stop by Da Vinci's before we hand him over to the cops."

"Hand me over?" Billy turned around to face Bird.

Bird jabbed his back with her knee.

Billy grunted. "You aren't cops either?"

"We're fugitive-recovery agents," Ruby said proudly.

"Aw, shit, bounty hunters? You dumb fucks have no idea what you just stepped in."

"We dumb fucks usually don't." Bird shoved his head back down on the floor.

•

Mr. V was saturated with sweat as he let his enforcer have it with both barrels. "You were right there. Right there!" He screamed at her, inches from her face.

"I'm sorry, sir," she said, unmoving, with no emotion in her voice.

The usually stoic bodyguards smirked at her. By and large she was so efficient that she made the men in the organization look bad, and they hated her for it. They knew better than to openly challenge her—even they had a healthy fear of Mr. V's top enforcer—so they always took pleasure in her failures, rare though they may be.

"Everything he knows about my finances . . . !" The crime lord breathed fire. Suddenly, as if he'd just remembered something important, he placed a hand over his heart. He closed his eyes, inhaled deeply, then exhaled. "If the feds get ahold of him, well, we had better all get used to smaller accommodations." He wiped the sweat from his face with a towel and continued breathing long, relaxing breaths. "Do we even know who took him? Maybe I can still pull some strings."

"It wasn't the cops," she said.

"Then who?"

"Bounty hunters. I ran across them on the Stiffe job."

"Ah, yes, as I recall, you failed to get me the money. Quite the track record you're building. At least you're consistent."

The bodyguards snorted openly now. This was the worst day she had ever had, and therefore their best. No doubt word would soon spread to every goon in the organization.

"I'll have Billy back before the day is over." She peered at the men out of the corner of her eye with a look that screamed murder. One of them, perhaps the wiser of the two, wiped the smirk off his face. But the other bodyguard, who had a shiny gold tooth, just kept smiling and winked at her. Goldie would eventually regret the move.

"I've had enough disappointment from you," Mr. V said.

"Sir, I can handle it." She tried to make eye contact to convey her sincerity. But the crime boss would not deign to meet her gaze; he turned his back to her.

"My boys will handle it."

His emphasis on the word *boys* did not go unnoticed. Her face flushed with the insult. "Sir, I assure you—"

"I said, they'll handle it!"

"Yes . . . sir."

9

SPONTANEOUS AND FUN, LIKE A CAR CRASH

VICKY DELICATELY DABBED AT one of her paintings. For some reason she always looked like she was figuring out a complex mathematical equation when she painted, her eyes squinted, her brow furrowed, and her tongue stuck out the side. Never mind that the finished product looked like a five year old had dipped his hands in paint and smeared the canvas. To Vicky it was a carefully calculated process.

Dippo filled out paperwork at his desk. Now and again he snuck a glance at Vicky. He smiled every time he saw her tongue poking out.

"So I tell Mochabean," Vicky said in between dabs, "I sent you after Thomas Trent. Mr. Trent is a man. What you brought back is a woman. You can tell the difference because of the two pointy things on her chest."

"Uh-huh, pointy," Dippo said.

"At least with Bird and Jesse I know what to expect. Don't tell those two misfits I said this, but I've grown somewhat fond of them."

Dippo looked up and arched an eyebrow. "I'm sure the feeling's mutual."

Vicky stretched in her wheelchair and groaned. She twisted

to get the kinks out of her back. Then she cracked her knuckles, a trait many people would find irritating—but not Dippo; he just grinned at the familiar popping sound.

"Can I interest you . . . ," Dippo took a deep breath, then continued tentatively, "in a foot massage?"

"What?" Vicky paused midstretch.

"It's, uh, for relieving tension. You seem like you could use it."

"You are aware that I'm in a wheelchair?" She pointed at one of the rubber wheels.

"It's OK. I can do it while you're sitting there. You don't have to get up." He stood and started walking toward her.

"Dippo, I can't feel anything from my waist down. I should think a foot massage would be wasted on me."

"Oh." Dippo slowly sat back down and buried his face in paperwork. "Never mind then. Sorry about that."

"Don't worry about it. But I do appreciate the thought."

Dippo blushed and dug his head even deeper into his paperwork, a vulnerable little animal making his escape from a fatally embarrassing situation. Something out of the ordinary had just transpired, something awkward. For the first time in her life Vicky was at a loss for words. Only the trademark squeal of Jesse's van broke the uncomfortable silence.

Bird and Ruby walked in arguing, which by now was their normal method of communication. Jesse and a handcuffed Billy Veach followed close behind. No one in the group seemed particularly happy, except of course for Jesse, who always walked around with a contented smile, like a modern-day but less rotund Buddha.

"I don't want to go to the zoo," Ruby complained. "I want to help you catch criminals like I did today. It was so spontaneous. It was awesome!"

Big sister stopped in her tracks, turned to Ruby. "Traffic

accidents are spontaneous. Do you see people buying tickets to get into one of those?"

"Stop treating me like a child." Ruby raised on her tiptoes, now face-to-face with Bird, who was a few inches taller.

"Then quit whining like you're seven years old." The sisters were nose-to-nose, neither one backing off. A common-enough occurrence when they were growing up together, but one that Bird had hoped they had outgrown. It was pointless. It was childish. And she sure as hell wasn't going to be the first to flinch.

Vicky rolled up between them, ending the standoff. "You got Veach already? This has to be a record. It only took you a week," she said sarcastically. "Next time take the case when I offer it, and we won't waste so much time dancing around."

Bird confronted Vicky. "We have unfinished business, Ms. Da Vinci."

Vicky slit her eyes. She got a nervous tic just under the left side of her mouth. It always did this when something was about to separate her from her money. "Business? What business? Get Veach to the county jail so I can get my money back."

Bird placed both hands on the wheelchair to make sure Vicky couldn't get away. "First we discuss my money. From the Stiffe job."

"I already took care of that. Didn't I? I must have." She avoided Bird's gaze and tried rolling away.

"No, you didn't." Bird put her full weight down on the chair. "Soon as you hand over my money, I drop off Veach at the jail."

"You're blackmailing me?" The look of hurt was not even remotely genuine. It didn't help that anyone who knew her for longer than five minutes soon realized Vicky Da Vinci was a penny-pinching skinflint. "Bird, this is so crass, so vulgar."

Bird simply rolled her eyes.

Ruby turned to Jesse. "Is it always this difficult to get paid in your line of work?"

"You kidding?" Jesse shook his head. "This is nothing. One time, she fell in the bathroom and hit her head on the sink. For a whole month she pretended to have amnesia. Every time we came around asking for our fee, she'd say, 'What money? Who are you people? I can taste colors.'"

"How did you know she was faking?" Ruby asked.

"Eventually, Bird got so fed up she threatened to help jog her memory with a lead pipe. After that, Vicky had what the doctors called a 'miraculous recovery.'" Jesse chuckled. "You can only push your sister so far."

"Just pay up already, you miser," Bird demanded.

"All right. OK," Vicky relented. "Just back off. And pop a Tic Tac, for God's sake."

Billy the accountant scoffed at the shoddy office and at the misfits who'd nabbed him right out from under his father's nose. Now that he knew his captors weren't sent by one of his dad's rivals, odds were good he probably wasn't going to get a bullet in the head. These were just low-rent bounty hunters, not even real cops. As such, he felt no need to hold his tongue. "You losers don't know what you're doing. You probably don't even know who I am."

"I know exactly what you are: one hundred thousand dollars of my bond money," Vicky growled at him.

"And 10 percent of that is mine," Bird interjected.

"Ten percent? Is that what we agreed to? I seem to recall it was 9." Her wheelchair broke free of Bird's grip, and Vicky rolled back to the safety of her desk.

"Jesus, you tightwad." Frustrated, Bird tugged at her own hair. She pulled it back into place immediately—no hair out of place.

"Pay close attention, now. I'm Billy Veach. Son of Robert Veach." He let that sink in for a second, perhaps expecting a bit of deference.

Ruby's eyes went wide, and she smiled. "Hey, it just hit me—this guy's a son of a Veach!" She snort-laughed, then quickly covered her mouth with her hand.

"What's wrong with you people?" Billy said. "Didn't you hear me? My dad's Robert Veach!"

"Robert who?" Jesse scratched at his head.

"Hold on a minute—Robert W. Veach?" Vicky said with sudden recognition.

"Finally, we got a live one," Billy said.

"What?" Bird asked. "Who's Robert W. Veach?"

"Robert W. Veach, the owner of the Party Palace chain stores?" Vicky asked.

"I strongly suggest you let me go now." Billy held up his handcuffed wrists.

"What?" Bird was growing impatient. "Who is this guy?" She knocked his arms down and forced him into a chair. Far as she could tell, this guy was just another white-collar criminal. She studied his face and wondered what the hell a "Party Palace" was.

"Bird, don't you watch the news?" Vicky said, exasperated.

"I don't need to know how screwed up the world is."

"Here, wait." Vicky dug through a pile of newspapers. She discarded several till she found the one she was looking for. She rolled over to Bird, held the paper up, and pointed at a story. Her finger was square on a black-and-white picture of a certain gym-obsessed mobster. Mr. V, a.k.a. "Robert W. Veach: suspected head of organized crime throughout the East Side. Questioned in the disappearance of half a dozen people."

"That's my dad, the magician, always making people vanish

into thin air when they displease him," Billy said sarcastically. "And I'm his accountant. I know 'things.' Things he doesn't want the feds to find out about. He won't stop till he gets me back. And he won't let anyone get in the way."

"Ha!" Ruby pointed a finger at Veach the younger. "Did you guys hear that? He practically just confessed to us. Do we get extra money for confessions? Oh, we must."

When the implications of this new information hit her, Bird's vision blurred. The room started to spin around her. As a cop, she'd dealt with everything from gangbangers to drug dealers, but in all that time she'd only ever fired her gun once at another human being. As a fugitive-recovery agent, the company hadn't gotten any classier, but she'd yet to fire a weapon. She always knew, worse come to worse, she could always walk away from this life, and that would be the end of it. No repercussions, no looking over her shoulder.

But this was the Mob, organized crime, Cosa Nostra, and they were good at holding a grudge. You mess around with this bunch, and you wind up with a horse head in your bed, or the entire horse carcass, or as a carcass yourself under the horse stables. What if they discovered she was the one who caught Billy Veach? What if they came after her? Who could she turn to for help? Not the police—her ex-partner happened to be the one person she'd ever fired a weapon at. He had tried to kill her first, when he discovered Bird had been having an affair with his wife, so really it was self-defense on Bird's part. Just the same, the police took a dim view of her actions and probably wouldn't come to her rescue anytime soon. Suddenly, her tongue felt like a hardened, dry sponge in her mouth.

Bird was just a private citizen now, and if this Robert Veach character did come after her, she wouldn't be missed by anyone but her family. Oh, God, Ruby! She had to look after Ruby on top of everything else. A cold fear traveled down her spine and turned her knees to rubber. She grabbed at the back of a chair for support. "I can't believe this. You sent us after the son of the fucking Godfather!"

Dippo quickly rose from his desk. "I'll just lock the front door then." He switched the knobs on three Deadbolts, then peeked out a window.

"I got the back, man." Jesse ambled away into Vicky's private office, where the rear exit was located.

"I—I had no idea," Vicky stammered. "Why would the son of Robert Veach come to me for bail? He didn't tell me any of this. Nothing about this was in the file!" She rolled over to Billy, grabbed him violently by the shirt, and yanked him down toward her. "Your father has buckets of money. Why did you have to get me involved in this, you little bastard?"

"It's all gone into legal bills," Billy said by way of apology. "He doesn't have much left. The lawyers are sucking him dry."

"He can't bail his own son out of jail? Doesn't sound like much of a gangster to me," Ruby snorted.

Billy shook his head at her naïveté. "He still has connections, with the local cops, with other guys 'in the business.'" He paused, considering his words carefully. "It was enough to take care of the prosecutor at his last trial."

Bird's nervous gulp was so loud it would have played as comical in any other situation. But not when she was the one about to be "taken care of." "What do you mean? What happened to the prosecutor?"

Billy's brow wrinkled, and he shook his head in the universal sign for "You don't want to know."

"Vicky?" Bird turned to the woman she blamed for her current predicament.

"Nobody knows. They haven't heard from him in two

months. Best-case scenario, he's hiding out somewhere. Worst case . . . " Vicky rolled into her private office.

Meanwhile, everyone else was witness to a rare treat. Bird's face worked its way through the entire color spectrum of paranoia: from sickly green to troubled gray to deathly white, all within seconds.

In her office, Vicky fumbled with the combination of a safe under her desk. Her fingers shook slightly, but otherwise she seemed composed. "Bird, I want you to get him to jail as fast as you possibly can in that heap you call a vehicle. Then I want you to get yourself and your sister out of the city. Consider it that vacation you're always whining about. I'll give you some money if you need."

Christ on a bike, Vicky Da Vinci is offering me money, Bird thought. This is worse than I thought. She turned a protective eye toward her baby sister, who didn't seem at all fazed. If anything, she had the barest hint of a crooked smile. She couldn't possibly think all this was fun . . .

"What, should we be worried?" Ruby said casually.

"Worried?" Bird answered, dripping with sarcasm. "I got the Mob after me. How's that for spontaneous? How's that for fun? Weee!"

"You know, Bird, maybe if you weren't such a bitch, bad things wouldn't happen to you," Ruby snapped back.

"And maybe if you'd stayed home, I wouldn't have to worry about you on top of everything else."

"I can take care of myself, I'll have you know."

"Oh, please, I've had to take care of you for years. Ruby needs a babysitter, Ruby needs a car, Ruby needs tuition money—it's a never-ending thing with you! I'm sick of having to look out for you all the time. I want a life of my own. You're a stone around my neck, girl, and you're dragging me down to a watery grave!"

Bird pulled at her collar to demonstrate.

The words stung Ruby visibly. Lord knows the two had fought before, but it usually wasn't so barbed, so personal. She had no ready reply to the accusation of being responsible for Bird's watery death, other than possibly "Am not!" And somehow that didn't seem strong enough.

Ruby turned to Dippo and Jesse for a lifeline. But neither of them offered any help; they knew better than to jump into the crossfire. That only left Ruby with the option to hold her tongue for the moment, which she reluctantly did.

When standing and screaming got to be too much strain, Bird sat in the chair she held for support. She placed her head down in her hands and sighed, waiting for the room to stop spinning. "Everyone just shut up for a moment. Let a woman think."

After a few minutes, Jesse lay on his back on the floor. It wasn't that strange a thing in and of itself. Even when he began pumping his arms and legs in the air like he was riding an invisible bike it was still barely within the realm of acceptable behavior. But when Jesse burst into boisterous laughter for no apparent reason, it was too much to handle.

"Have you finally lost what little is left of your mind?" Bird snapped.

"It's laughasan," Jesse said cheerily. "A yoga breathing technique that fights off anger and sadness. Come, join me. Ha, ha, ha!" He cackled like a madman.

Bird groaned at the absurdness. "I am not getting on that filthy floor, you lunatic."

A bounty hunter in the midst of mental breakdown, a girl barely out of diapers, and a hippie—these are the people who had captured Billy Veach, son of one of the most dangerous crime lords in L.A. County. Billy shook his head, perhaps in disappointment, at the scene before him. Then he looked out the front window, and his blood ran cold.

Parked across the street in her dark sedan was Mr. V's female enforcer, bringer of death and destruction. She smiled and made a shooting gesture at Billy.

"I knew it," he mumbled. "This time she'll kill me for sure. I'm outta here." He ran past everyone into Vicky's private office and slammed the door closed behind him.

"Hey!" Bird called out.

Then something shattered the window. A dark cylindrical object the size of a can of beans rolled to the middle of the room. It got everyone's attention and waited patiently for someone to comment.

Bird sighed, "Aw, crap."

Thick white smoke hissed out of the cylinder, quickly filling the office with a choking haze.

"Smoke grenade—cover your mouths!" Bird yelled. She fumbled around on her knees, trying to locate the grenade. There was a chance she could still throw it back out. All around her, people coughed and hacked as they ran into each other. Just as Bird got her hand on the smoke grenade, Jesse stumbled over her, knocked it out of her palm, and fell to the ground.

As everyone struggled to get their bearings in the miasma, the front door flew off its hinges. Two men wearing gas masks strode in. They pointed large handguns at Bird and her friends and sister. She couldn't identify what sort of guns they were, but she suspected anyone who resorted to throwing military smoke grenades into a person's office could probably afford top-of-the-line weaponry as well.

Since she was closest to the door, Bird could make out that one of the men had a bowl haircut, the kind you only ever saw on "special needs" children, or Moe from the Three Stooges.

Fittingly, the other man was bald like Curly. Even in the face of danger, Bird couldn't help herself, she had to wonder, Huh, what about Larry?

"Where is he?" Moe yelled from behind his mask.

"Where's who?" Jesse said, then broke into a fit of coughing.

Moe grabbed Jesse's shirt, shoved a gun under his chin. "Don't fuck with us, burnout. Where is he?"

Curly waved his gun around the room. "Anyone moves, everyone dies."

Ruby was the first to ignore their commands—no surprise there. She stumbled about, looking for her sister, and rubbed at her face. "Bird, my eyes burn!"

Bird stopped hacking out a lung long enough to yell, "Breathe through your shirt." She brusquely lifted up the collar of Ruby's shirt.

"I can do it myself!" Ruby pushed her hand away.

"All right, then do it!"

In the midst of an all-out assault by armed strangers, the Blacker sisters were going at each other like rabid weasels.

Moe still had Jesse by the scruff. "I said, where is he?" When Jesse stared back at him with confused, bloodshot eyes, Moe struck him across the face with the gun, knocking Jesse to the ground.

•

In her private office, Vicky was still fumbling with her personal safe. "What was the last number?" Her fingers shook uncontrollably. She squeezed them together tightly to stop the trembling.

Only then did she notice Billy Veach, cowering behind her

desk. He pulled and yanked at the handcuffs on his wrist, to no avail.

"What's going on out there?" Vicky said. "They're here for you, aren't they?"

"She's fucking crazy." Like a trapped and hunted animal, he looked around for any available escape route. "You don't know. My father hates failure. He won't tolerate it, from anyone. You don't know. Oh, God, help me."

"Get out there and help," she commanded. "Tell them to stop. Tell them it was a misunderstanding. Go with them. I don't care, but do something."

Shaky as Vicky's fingers were, they had nothing on Billy, who quivered from head to toe with fear. "She's gonna kill me this time. She's always wanted to, and now she's going to do it. Jesus, she'll just say I got hit by a stray bullet. Jesus, oh, Jesus."

"You're useless," Vicky spat out in disgust. She turned to the safe, her fingers now motionless with a new sense of purpose. "The last number is . . . forty-nine!" She quickly spun the dial on the safe.

•

Outside in the main office, Dippo covered his mouth with a white handkerchief and pointed at the closed door to Vicky's office. "He's in there. Just take him and don't hurt anyone, please."

"Finally," Moe said, "some common sense." He dropped Jesse and strode across the office.

Bird helped Jesse to his feet, and, looking around to make sure no one was watching, she grabbed an apple-shaped paperweight off a desk. Even if Moe or Curly had seen her take it, the heavy fruit was painted a shiny red and resembled real produce. An apple a day may threaten the medical profession, but it presented little risk to a couple of armed men.

"You OK?" Bird asked her pacifist partner.

Jesse's eyes were still bloodshot, but he had recovered enough of his senses to answer. "It's just my face. All of it."

Curly turned to best pal Moe. "Watch them," he said.

Moe grinned as he pointed his weapon at Bird and Jesse. "We understand each other?"

"Sure, I understand." But look away for even a second, and I'll wipe that smirk off your bowl-headed, retarded-looking face, you jackass, Bird thought.

Curly was having trouble getting into Vicky's private office. It was locked tight. "Open up in there." He banged on the door, kicked at it, twisted the knob. "I said—"

Ka-blam!—a gunshot from inside the office blew away a chunk of the door inches from Curly's face. Splinters clobbered him with such force that it cracked open his mask. He went down screaming like a banshee.

Then the door swung open, and out rolled Vicky Da Vinci holding the biggest damn gun since Clint Eastwood's day was made. "Who else wants some?" she screamed. "Kiss the cook, you sons-a-bitches!"

With one intruder clawing at his face on the floor and the other distracted, Bird made her move. She smashed Moe on the head with the heavy apple paperweight. The man dropped instantly, a puppet with his strings cut. "Get their guns!" Bird yelled out, as she handcuffed the men.

Jesse and Ruby scrambled around and quickly recovered the firearms before either man could recover. Tears streaked the younger Blacker sister's face, and Jesse's legs had not completely solidified, but even so, they'd come out on the winning side. They smiled at each other and high-fived.

"Anybody hurt?" Bird looked directly at her sister when she asked.

Ruby wiped the tears from her face. "I'm OK."

"I'll live," Jesse said.

"Just peachy creamy," Dippo said, still behind his desk.

Bird glared at Vicky, who gripped her enormous gun in both hands and seemed eager to fire off another round. "What if one of us had been standing by that door?"

"Don't you judge me." She held up the firearm. "Big Bertha and I just saved all your hides."

"By shooting from behind a closed door?" Bird demanded. "Silly me, why didn't I just pull my piece and blast away in the middle of a smoke-filled room?"

"I didn't hit anyone, did I?"

"By sheer grace of God," Bird said, mad as hell.

"But I didn't, did I? No, I didn't. So zip it up, before I zip it for you." Vicky was not in the habit of backing down from an argument, especially not when she was holding the biggest gun in the room. "Remember, I got plenty more ammo," she said by way of a barely veiled threat.

The two women stared at each other with murderous gazes, neither one giving ground. Fortunately, cooler heads prevailed.

"Ahem, has anyone seen Billy?" Ruby asked.

Grudgingly, Vicky turned away. "The little creep was hiding under my desk."

Dippo walked out of the private office. "Well, he's not in there anymore. He must've slipped out the back."

Bird sighed, unsure if she should be pissed at losing a skip or glad to be rid of Billy Veach and the added turmoil he'd brought into her life. She cuffed a moaning Curly and an unconscious Moe to a pipe on the wall. At least neither of them would be going anywhere for the time being. "He's probably halfway to Mexico by now."

Without a moment's second thought, Ruby ran out the door. "I'll check out front for him."

"Ruby, wait, don't!" Bird couldn't believe her sister's impetuous nature. They'd just been besieged, gassed, and shot at, and the girl runs out like she was off to meet her friends at the mall. "Dammit, what's it take to get her to listen?"

"Must run in the family," Vicky said.

10

HELL ON WHEELS

THE ENFORCER WAITED CALMLY in her Lincoln Town Car, parked across the street from Da Vinci Bail Bonds. She focused like a laser on the front of the office, waiting to see how the situation played out. She wasn't supposed to be here—her boss made it abundantly clear he wanted his "boys" to handle the matter—but she'd tailed them nonetheless. It's a good thing she had too, as both men had proven themselves completely ineffectual.

"Looks like the boys couldn't handle the job." Through the dissipating smoke, she saw Bird handcuffing both of Mr. V's men to the wall. This was her chance to prove herself to the crime lord. She smiled when she saw Ruby walk out of the office all by her lonesome. "Christmas came early this year."

The Lincoln rumbled to life as the enforcer gunned the engine. The car screeched to a halt in front of Ruby, forcing her to jump back onto the sidewalk to avoid becoming roadkill.

"Jeez, you almost hit me, you maniac!" the girl screamed at the black-tinted driver's window.

Slowly, the window rolled down to reveal the long barrel of a gun aimed dead center at Ruby. The weapon had a silencer screwed on at the end, making it that much more menacing.

"Whoa." Ruby backed away. "Never mind. It was totally my fault."

"Get in," the driver commanded.

Ruby took a step back toward the office door. A single shot ricocheted at the girl's feet. Ruby froze in place. The safety of the office was five feet away. She saw the driver's chilly smile, daring her to try to make a run for it. "OK . . . " Ruby clambered into the Lincoln.

In that instant, Vicky rolled out the front door and caught sight of Ruby getting into the car. "Where the devil are you going?"

"Vicky, help!" Ruby cried out. The driver reached out and yanked Ruby into the car. The Lincoln's wheels spun and burned rubber.

"No you don't!" Vicky dashed for the car and managed to grab onto the rear bumper a millisecond before the Lincoln peeled off.

Bird and Jesse ran out in time to see the car whiplash Vicky away. She rolled behind the Lincoln in her wheelchair, the seat wobbling dangerously side to side.

It was an extraordinary sight to behold, Vicky's wheelchair attached to the rear of a speeding sedan, but to her credit, Bird reacted calmly and quickly. "In the van—let's go." She grabbed Jesse's arm and lugged him behind her.

"Hang on, Vicky!" Jesse called out to his suddenly speedy employer.

•

The enforcer drove with one hand on the wheel, the other on her gun. She looked over at the unwilling passenger next to her. "What's your name?"

"Fuck you." Ruby stared straight ahead.

The older woman waited exactly two seconds—perhaps to give Ruby a false sense of security?—then she lashed out ruthlessly and smacked the girl across the cheek. "Pleased to meet you."

Ruby spat out blood and her eyes teared up, but she didn't so much as whimper. She did, however, deliver a bloodcurdling glare to her captor.

But the coldhearted killer was long past the days when looks from her victims—no matter how intense—had any effect on her. "See what being difficult gets you?" In any other setting the tone of her voice could have been considered friendly, her smile almost human. "You don't fight someone stronger than you head-on. You outsmart them."

•

Jesse hunched over the steering wheel of his van, his eyes glued to Vicky's wheelchair far ahead in the road. They were quickly gaining ground on the Lincoln.

Bird shook her head in disbelief at the sight of Vicky holding onto the car's bumper for dear life. "That woman is a certifiable lunatic. Get us closer."

"You got it." Just ahead, a man in handcuffs ran down the sidewalk. "Hey, check that out."

Billy Veach ran like a man possessed. He looked over his shoulder, his expression easy to read: he was running for his life. In fact, he was so concerned with who could be following him that he didn't notice when the door flew open on a parked pickup ahead of him. He turned and slammed into it face-first and bounced off with a metallic Clang!

Mochabean the giant lumbered out of the truck. He picked up the dazed Billy with one hand, like the average person would lift a bag of groceries. As Jesse's van drove past, Mochabean flipped Bird the bird and grinned a yellow smile at them. He was finally getting payback for Bird stealing one of his skips.

"What do you want to do—should I stop?" Jesse asked.

"No," Bird said. "Let Mochabean deal with the Sopranos if he wants. You stay with Da Vinci."

They sped past and were soon pulling up behind the Lincoln. Under normal circumstances Jesse's van wouldn't have been able to catch up, but the Lincoln's driver was overconfident and had not yet noticed her pursuers.

Bird stuck her body out the passenger-side window and yelled at Vicky, who clung for life to the bumper. "What are you doing? Let go of the car!"

Unfortunately, the combination of distance and a preoccupation with not dying made it difficult for Vicky to clearly hear. "What?" she said.

"The car, let go of the car!" Bird yelled at the top of her lungs.

The chair hit a bump in the road and almost flipped. Vicky's face went white as the wheels wobbled and the chair quivered madly over the speeding asphalt. She gritted her teeth and grabbed on tighter. "They have your sister!"

"What?" It seemed Bird was having her own auditory troubles—what with the wind rushing at her face as she hung out of a speeding van and all. She thought she heard something about Vicky having a blister.

She called to her partner in the van. "Jesse, get me closer."

The van swerved toward the wheelchair, and Bird almost fell out the passenger window. She glared at Jesse. "Slowly!"

"Sorry," he said sheepishly. "That was my fault. That was me."

Bird reached out with one hand. "Let go! You're gonna get killed!"

"They. Have. Ruby!" Vicky enunciated and nodded at the car.

"Ruby?" And finally it registered loud and clear: her sister was in danger. With a sudden sense of burning guilt, Bird realized she hadn't even thought about Ruby's whereabouts since she ran out the door. She'd just seen Vicky yanked away and had given chase. It never occurred to her that Ruby might be involved. Some big sister she was.

Bird looked ahead and saw Ruby's face in the car's side rearview mirror. The girl's lip was bleeding.

The bounty hunter ducked back into the van. "They have Ruby in that car. We have to stop it. No matter what."

"How we gonna do that, man?" Jesse asked. "You—you don't want me to ram it, do you?" If asked, he would probably do it to save a friend, but damaging his van further would be like giving up a kidney.

"Keep us steady." She pulled out her handgun from a shoulder holster. Bird didn't like the idea of using firearms if there was a chance of her sister getting hurt, but she didn't see any other option. "I'm going to shoot out one of their tires."

"No way, for real? Like on TV?"

Why not? If they could do it on television, that meant it was possible, didn't it? Bird gulped down all her doubts, and any remaining common sense that might still be hanging around, then she once again leaned her body out the passenger window. She took careful aim at the rear car tire farthest from Vicky and her wheelchair. Fortunately, both Vicky and Ruby were on the same side of the car. That left Bird the entire driver's side of the car to shoot at.

"You sure about this, Ladybird?" Jesse didn't seem so calm or zenlike anymore. Beads of nervous sweat gathered on his forehead.

"No problem. I can do this." She dearly hoped she sounded confident.

Less than twenty feet ahead, Vicky turned and caught

sight of Bird aiming a gun in her general direction. She was, understandably, concerned. "Son of a bitch! What are you doing?" she cried out into the rushing wind.

And although Bird could not make out her words exactly, she got the general gist.

•

In the Lincoln Town Car, the driver looked in the rearview and finally noticed the beat-up van trailing behind. "Look at that, we picked up a parade," she said to her hostage.

From inside the car, it was impossible to see the crazy woman in a wheelchair tenaciously hanging onto the rear of the Lincoln. As far as they knew, it was only the van back there.

Hope flashed across Ruby's face when she saw Bird and company bringing up the rear. Her big sister had gotten her out of scrapes throughout all her life, and surely this would be no different.

Almost as if she was reading Ruby's mind, the enforcer took steps to quash any delusions of the cavalry coming to the rescue. She jerked the steering wheel to the right and slammed on the gas.

This had two immediate effects: it made the wheelchair swerve even more erratically, and it threw off Bird's careful aim. Instead of puncturing the car's tire and ending the madcap car chase, the bullet ricocheted off Vicky's armrest, causing her left hand to release the car bumper. She flailed about for a second, her right hand barely hanging on, before she was able to regain her grip with both hands.

"For the love of God!" she screamed at Bird. "Put the gun away!" Even with the wind blowing in Bird's face, this time it was easy to grasp the point Vicky was trying to get across.

"Damn it, I said keep us steady, Jesse!" Bird adjusted her position and, undeterred, once again took aim at the car tire.

•

The Lincoln's driver heard the bullet hit, and she could see Bird leveling a gun at them. "All right then, let's escalate," she said, and pulled her own piece. She aimed her gun out the driver's side window with the natural ease of someone who did this several times a week.

"Don't!" Ruby cried out when she saw her sister was in danger. She pummeled the woman in the face with two quick elbow jabs, catching her off-guard.

The enforcer dropped her gun out the window. The weapon rattled down the street, firing once as it bounced on the pavement.

The stray bullet hit a corner of the van's windshield and cracked the glass. "Whoa!" Jesse ducked down in the driver's seat. "Evasive maneuvers!" He turned the steering wheel left and right, in an effort to make the cumbersome vehicle harder to hit. But in doing so he forgot to warn Bird. She bounced around the window, her gun waving wildly, as she tried to regain her balance.

To Vicky, who had almost been the victim of Bird's unimpressive marksmanship, seeing the bounty hunter waving her gun around did not inspire confidence. "Lord, help me," she sighed. "Death by imbeciles."

Jesse's weaving maneuvers were so drastic—he wanted no more bullet holes in his baby—that Bird almost fell out the window. She floundered around like a rag doll and hit the side of the window with a loud Crack!

"Uhn!" Bird grunted. There goes a rib. Something was

definitely broken, but at least she found a grip and pulled herself back into the van.

•

In the Lincoln, Ruby's love of martial arts had served her well; she was holding her own against the seasoned killer who'd taken her hostage. She got in at least two good strikes and had a clump of the woman's hair in her fist. It didn't hurt that the driver had to steady the car with one hand while blocking Ruby's blows with the other.

"Crazy bitch!" she snarled after Ruby kicked her in the head.

The enforcer let go of the steering wheel, roared like some sort of injured beast, and slammed Ruby across the jaw, sending her off to a fuzzy, dark world. She must have thought that was the end of it, because she turned back to the road ahead. But she underestimated her lively hostage.

Even on the edge of blacking out, Ruby would not quit, especially now that her captor didn't have a gun to threaten her with. Woozy and half-blind, the girl lashed out like a wildcat, all fists and fingers and teeth, in a feral assault.

The Lincoln swerved down the street out of control as the driver tried to hold back the creature that had pounced on her. Behind them, the wheelchair whiplashed violently back and forth. Finally, the killer got in a good shot—Ruby's head snapped back and hit the window. This time she was out for sure.

It was too much. Vicky had managed to hold on now for several miles; she'd even survived being shot at by her would-be rescuers. But this forceful jerking to and fro was more than she could handle, no matter how badly she wanted to hang on.

Vicky's fingers burned from the strain, the tendons in her hands strained to the breaking point, until finally, with an agonizing "No-o-o!" her hands slipped away and she rolled back toward the van.

But instead of running over her, the van turned at the last second and came up beside Vicky's wheelchair. The side door slid open and Bird reached out. When they clasped hands, she pulled Vicky into the van. Meanwhile, the empty wheelchair flipped away into oncoming traffic. Vicky and Bird tumbled awkwardly into the vehicle and crashed against Jesse.

"Watch out," he said, as they shoved him and he lost control of the wheel. His beloved van was not exactly agile under the best of circumstances, but at this speed and with the steering wheel spinning free, it was the perfect combination to send them into a wild 360-degree spin down the street.

Everyone inside followed proper protocol for just such a situation: they screamed for their lives.

•

Officer Bonaventura was on a roll. This was the tenth car he'd ticketed on this street so far. His personal best was thirteen in a row, and it looked like he might break the record today.

In Los Angeles you can park legally on a street only to return and discover you got a ticket because parking there is no longer allowed after six o'clock, or on a Monday, or overnight, or during a full moon in the merry month of May. In fact, the only thing more frustrating than navigating L.A. traffic is trying to find a place to park once you get to your destination.

"Oh-ho," Officer Bonaventura said triumphantly as he wrote a ticket to a Toyota Camry parked facing the wrong direction. "This one has an expired sticker on top of everything else. If only all crime fighting was this easy."

Suddenly, a dark Lincoln blew past the policeman and down the street. Then he heard a strange squealing noise coming up from behind. When he turned his eyes bulged with fear. A spinning van bore down on him at an incredible speed. He had no time to move out of harm's way.

•

Jesse untangled himself from the mess of arms and legs that were pinning him down. He reached out and pumped the brakes. The van screeched loudly as it skidded, the tires smoked, and the smell of burning rubber was everywhere. Finally, they came to a lurching halt.

Bird was the first to regain her bearings. She looked out the front windshield to assess the situation. "Jesse?" she said in a hoarse whisper.

"Yeah?"

"I suggest you get us out of here. Fast."

Out the windshield they saw a policeman cringing and covering his face with his hands. They had nearly crushed him between the van and a Toyota behind him. If Jesse hadn't hit the brakes exactly when he did, the cop would have been paste.

After several terror-filled seconds, Officer Bonaventura lowered his hands. He saw the van drive off, but couldn't make out any of the passengers. He patted his legs to make sure they were still there. He was relieved to find they were, and trembling uncontrollably. Then he collapsed to the ground.

•

They had been searching for the Town Car a good hour and a half now, with no luck. They'd lost track of it for only a few seconds—when the van did its Ice Capades routine—but that was all it needed to escape.

Bird glanced up and down the streets as they drove along. "See anything?"

"No dice, man," said Jesse. "That car is long gone."

Bird angrily slammed her fist on the van's dashboard. The Polaroid picture Ruby had taken of them jumped out of its nook and hung at an angle on the dash. It looked like a smiling Ruby was holding on as a frowning Bird was trying to pull her back to safety.

"Hey, hey, hey, man!" Jesse said defensively. "Take it easy on my baby. She's already been wounded today."

In the back, Vicky sat on the floor now that her wheelchair was gone. They hadn't even had time to go looking for it yet, and she hadn't brought it up. No doubt she felt uncomfortable having completely lost mobility, but finding Ruby came first, as far as everyone was concerned.

Still, there were other ways for people to express their frustration. "Oh, for the love of . . . " Vicky said, frowning. "I've seen Lego towers hold together better than this van of yours."

"Man, your negativity is not what the situation calls for," Jesse scolded.

"And I suppose chanting would be of some use?"

"Sarcasm is a hidden form of hostility, man."

"I assure you there's nothing hidden about my hostility."

"You're darkening everyone's karmic space, man."

"Stuff your karmic space," Vicky said irately. "And stop calling me 'man,' you twit."

Jesse drove in silence for a few moments. The victory in this verbal sparring match seemingly went to Da Vinci. Then Jesse came back with a fine flourish. "Anger makes your ass fat," he told her, grinning mischievously.

"You bleary-eyed buffoon, how dare you!" Vicky bellowed. Using only her arms, she dragged herself toward Jesse, murder in her eyes. "I'll twist your scrawny chicken neck!"

"Hey, no fair," he said. "I can't hit a cripple."

"I'm no cripple, you son of a—"

"Everyone shut up!" Bird yelled. Her cell phone had been ringing since the middle of the argument, but she'd only now heard it. The screen was cracked, having taken a blow when Bird was bouncing around the van's window. Her ribs were in one piece, but the phone wasn't long for this world. "What?" she said into the phone. "I'm having trouble hearing you."

"Where are you?" Dippo's voice said on the other side. "Is Vicky with you? Is she OK?"

"She's fine."

"The cops came. They took . . . other two . . . who called." The phone popped and hissed with static.

"What? What did you say?" Bird's frustration was growing exponentially.

"I said the police came!"

"Who the hell called the police? I wanted to squeeze those two for info."

" . . . just showed up . . . " The phone crackled one last time, then died.

"Hello? Dippo? You there?"

Even the damned cell phone had turned against her tonight. Enraged, Bird pounded it on the dashboard as she shrieked, "Just do your damned job!" Bam! "Why won't things work like they're supposed to!" Bam, bam! "Nothing ever works around here!" Bam, bam, bam!

By the time she was finished punishing the device, it was

missing half its buttons and it's high-tech guts spilled from dozens of cracks in the plastic. It had made the mistake of failing Bird Blacker in a moment of need. It would not live to repeat it. With a final grunt, Bird threw the broken phone out the window.

Vicky backed away from Jesse and sat between the front seats. Suddenly, throttling him wasn't such a pressing matter. Besides, he'd probably piss her off again soon enough. She could kill him then.

Any sage advice Jesse may have had for Bird, he wisely decided to keep to himself for the time being.

Ruby was gone, and she had no other course to follow at the moment, so Bird fell back on what she knew best. She squirted disinfectant on her hands and rubbed them vigorously. Dear God, they have my sister, she thought. What am I going to do now? She stared into her scrubbed hands looking for an answer, but there was none there to find. "I should've sent her home," she said forlornly.

"Come on, you can't blame yourself for the actions of deviants," Jesse reassured her.

Bird couldn't stop staring at her hands. She rubbed them violently, till they were red and raw, certain that if she got them clean enough they would offer up a solution to her problems.

"Bird?" Vicky put a hand on her arm to stop her from rubbing the skin off.

This was the closest to tears anyone had ever seen the tough ex-cop. She shook her head over and over. "She's my baby sister."

Jesse reached over and put a reassuring hand on Bird's reddened palm. Normally, she would cringe at the thought of holding Jesse's hand—every one of his fingernails had dirt and grime under them, every single one of them—but she let it slide this time. The feel of his hand on hers wasn't so bad right then. It didn't feel disgusting at all.

11

IT'S ONLY FUN TILL SOMEONE GETS KIDNAPPED

THE MAIN WAREHOUSE OF the Party Palace chain of stores was the stuff of children's dreams. Sacks and boxes and crates of bright balloons, candies of every form and flavor, and other colorful treats for festive occasions filled the building to nearly bursting.

In the middle of these jolly surroundings Ruby sat tied to a chair, dried blood on her face.

Her kidnapper kneeled by the girl and playfully slapped Ruby's face till she started to come around. As she spoke, the woman rubbed her own jaw, which had an ugly purple bruise where Ruby had hammered her good. "You got a solid kick. I can respect that."

Ruby blinked and swung her head lazily, like she'd been sedated. Frankly, the numbing effects of drugs would have been more than welcome right about then. "Where am I?" she mumbled.

"In deep shit. Keep quiet and you might still make it out in one piece." The enforcer smiled. Instead of reassuring them, this strange phenomenon actually had the effect of making people feel more ill at ease.

She walked to a small office, where Goldie, one of Mr. V's personal bodyguards, opened the door in mock chivalry. She pointedly ignored the large brute as she walked past.

Ruby shook the cobwebs—make that the buzzing hornets' nest—from her head and examined her surroundings. The first thing that caught her attention was the dozens of piñatas in the shapes of animals and cartoon characters, hung all along the ceiling. The papier-mâché creatures grinned down at her from every corner of the room. Ruby sighed. "I'm so screwed."

She heard her captor's voice in the office but couldn't see who she was talking to. It sounded like she was on the phone.

"Mr. V? I have the girl . . . ," the woman said, barely concealing the pride she felt.

Since nobody was watching her, Ruby took the opportunity to try to work loose the ropes holding her prisoner. Ruby could barely wiggle her fingers, let alone get enough slack to free herself. Whoever strapped her down knew a thing or two about tying a knot.

Ruby could see the woman's silhouette in the office window pacing back and forth.

"Yes, sir. At the East Side store. She put up quite a fight."

"You bet I did," Ruby muttered. She was still trying to get some leverage in the ropes, any small amount of slack so she could work on the knots. "Maybe some adrenaline will help me Hulk out of this." She took short, quick breaths, like she was hyperventilating, and gnashed her teeth. Then she flexed every muscle in her body and tried to burst out of her ropes, her face burning red from the effort. But, of course, she could not break the bonds. She didn't even loosen the ropes.

"Bird would know what to do." She looked up at the piñatas

again, their grins almost as menacing as her captor's. "This isn't fun anymore."

"I understand, Mr. V. I'll be there in ten minutes." In the office, the woman turned to the bodyguard with the gold tooth. "He wants you to stay here and take care of the girl."

"I'll take real good care of her," Goldie said, practically drooling with anticipation. "Don't you worry."

"Pig." She threw the phone at him as she walked out of the office.

Ruby trained her gaze on the enforcer as she walked up. The woman in the tailored suit knelt and grabbed Ruby's face. "You have your sister's eyes," she said as she studied Ruby's features.

"What?" the puzzled girl said.

And like a fickle child who's suddenly lost interest in an old toy, the woman stood and walked toward the exit. "Well, good-bye, slugger. Try to think happy thoughts."

After the door slammed, Ruby turned and saw the body-guard's shadow moving around in the office. Soon enough, he'd come sniffing around and she'd be in no position to swat him away.

"Hey, you out there," Goldie called out gruffly. "I gotta take a piss, but when I come back we'll have us some fun." He chuckled.

There was nobody coming to her rescue in the foreseeable future, and Ruby was stuck alone in this nasty situation. Nervously, she licked her lips. She wrinkled her nose as if tasting something sour. A small river of blood ran down from her nose into her mouth. Then she smiled, and you could almost see the lightbulb going on above her head as she formulated a plan.

She ran her tongue around the inside of her cheeks, mulling over her strategy. For a second her features darkened with concern. Then she took a deep breath and exhaled slowly. "OK . . . here goes."

She bit down hard on the inside of her cheek. The pain must have been intense, as tears welled up in her eyes. But she didn't cry or even whimper; instead, she bit down on the other side of her cheek. Her face contorted in agony. Tears streamed down her face. But still she did not cry out.

Ruby swirled the blood around in her mouth. She dripped the thick, gooey mixture down between her legs. Silent tears streamed down her cheeks. It took her a moment to compose herself for the next part.

"Hey, you," she called to the bodyguard in the office. "I have to use the bathroom!"

"Yeah, I'm gonna fall for that one," he said sarcastically.

"I really do."

"Shut up" was his curt response.

"Please!"

"I'm sorry—shut the fuck up."

"It hurts, you dumb ape!"

Goldie came out of the office zipping up his fly. "I told you to cut your shit." He saw her face marked with tears. "What?"

"I'm on my period," Ruby whimpered.

"So?"

Ruby looked down, and the bodyguard followed her gaze. A red puddle of blood pooled between her open legs. Now, any woman—hell, anyone even halfway paying attention—could tell that puddle of blood had nothing to do with menstruation, especially since it was on the outside of Ruby's pants, and not, as common sense would dictate, on the inside. Ruby, however, was perhaps counting on the man's distaste for both "feminine problems" and for common sense.

Goldie didn't disappoint. Soon as he saw the blood his nose

crinkled in revulsion and he took a step back, as if a woman's menstrual cycle was somehow contagious.

"Aw, man, that's, that's . . . You sick, little . . . " Words failed him.

"Look," Ruby said through her sobs, "I didn't plan this, all right? I wasn't expecting to get kidnapped today. It's only going to get worse unless I take care of it. I need to use the bathroom."

Repulsed as he was, the bodyguard looked suspicious. He probably hadn't gotten to his spot on the criminal food chain by being sensitive to his victims' needs.

"Oh, God, the cramps." Ruby twisted up her face in pain and cried even louder. She was really laying it on thick now. "I feel more blood coming. It's a heavy flow for sure!"

That was too much for Goldie, who still had to spend the rest of the day with this hostage. Shaking his head, he finally relented. "Jesus, all right, go put a cork in or something. But you better not give me any trouble."

He went behind the chair to untie her, but stayed at arm's length, still trying to avoid catching a case of the menses.

"I promise. No trouble." Ruby smiled a bloody smile.

12

TIME FOR PLAN B

DA VINCI BAIL BONDS had definitely seen better days. The front door hung on by a hinge, while the door to Vicky's private office now featured a decorative window, courtesy of her gun, Big Bertha. The smoke from the grenade had dissipated, but the odor lingered in the air. Meanwhile, furniture and paperwork lay strewn all over the place. And that's how Bird and her friends felt after the day's events: broken, smelly, and out-of-sorts.

As Dippo and Jesse went about cleaning up the office—Dippo methodically, Jesse not so much—Bird talked on an office phone with one of the kidnappers. She'd only been on with them for less than a minute, but already the veins bulged on her forehead. "Yeah, I got it . . . I said I got it!" she yelled at the receiver. "Let me talk to her. Hello? Hello? Bastard!"

She was about to smash the receiver, much as she had done with her own cell phone, when Vicky interjected. "Bird!"

"What?" She held the receiver high, ready for the downward strike.

Vicky rolled up in her now very dented wheelchair and held out her hand. "What did they say?"

"Sorry." Bird sighed, then placed the receiver in Vicky's palm. It was her phone after all. "They want to trade Billy for Ruby. If we tell the cops, they said they'll . . . "

She didn't need to finish. Besides, they already suspected the police. When Dippo called to inquire about the two men who'd attacked them earlier, the desk sergeant at the local precinct said he had no record of the men being arrested. Either it wasn't cops who carried them off, or, perhaps even worse, they were cops of the not-so-sterling variety. Bird couldn't take that chance. They were on their own on this one.

Everyone in the small office was apprehensive, scared, and irritable because of their present predicament. Everyone except Jesse. With his back on the floor, he raised both legs up against a wall, then inhaled deep, calm breaths. "Dude, we don't have Billy to trade. Mochabean took him, remember?"

Bird paced back and forth in the office. "They don't know we don't have him. Maybe we can bluff our way through this."

"Lies serve only to darken the path to wisdom, man." Jesse closed his eyes, breathed deeply.

"Lying to these kind of people is a dangerous game, Bird," Vicky warned. "You sure you want to go that route?"

"I'm doing the best I can here," the exhausted bounty hunter barked. "If anyone has a better idea, by all means, lay it on me." She waited.

Having no better plan, Dippo and Vicky looked at the floor.

"OK then." Bird continued pacing.

"I got an idea," Jesse said. Eyes still closed, he lifted his pelvis off the ground and pushed his legs farther up the wall.

Bird barely registered his existence, let alone any harebrained ideas that may have popped into his head. "Here's how it's going down," she said.

"I said I got an idea." Jesse was almost standing on his head now, with his legs far up the wall.

Paying him no mind, Bird continued, "We need someone about the same height and body type as Billy . . . "

"Acknowledge my thoughts as an individual, man," Jesse whined from his upside-down position.

"What is it? Can't you see the grownups are talking here?" Bird stopped pacing as she caught sight of Jesse upside down against the wall. She knew he was an odd duck; she'd learned to accept it. Yet he still had a knack for throwing her for a loop at the least-opportune moments. "You're standing on your head. Why is this?" She ran a hand down her frustrated face. Note to self, she thought: When this is all over, look for a new partner.

"It's called Legs of the Wall. It helps make the mind clear and encourages creativity," he said and opened his eyes. "It also prevents yeast infections."

"Yeast infections? Is that a problem for you?" Addendum to note: Forget partners altogether. From now on, work solo.

Jesse flipped over from his yoga stance and stood up straight, not a sign of yeast infections on him. "Why don't we steal Billy Veach back from Mochabean?"

"Because," Bird said as if speaking to a very young, very slow child, "Mochabean's already turned him in for a bounty. That's why we are called bounty hunters. Try to stay on this astral plane."

"No, he didn't, man." Jesse grinned from ear to ear.

"Jesse, if you can't help, then just be quiet. You're only being useless now."

"No, think about it, man. If Mochabean already turned him in, why hasn't he come for his bounty?" He held his hands out and cocked his head to the side quizzically.

"Because," Bird started—but she couldn't finish the sentence. She tried to find the fault in Jesse's stupid argument, normally an easy-enough task, yet this time she came up empty.

In fact, Jesse's rare use of logic stunned everyone into silence.

Neither Dippo nor Vicky could contradict him either.

Jesse continued, "Vicky put up the bail bond, didn't she? Mochabean has to come here to collect. I'm looking around, I don't see no big, bald mo-fo anywhere." He spun around to demonstrate.

"The dingbat's correct," said Vicky. "If he did turn Billy over to the police, Mochabean should've been here by now demanding his 15 percent."

"Fifteen percent?" Bird turned to Vicky, outraged. She could barely get 9 percent out of Vicky for recovering a bail skip, and she was giving that idiot Mochabean 15 percent? On top of everything else that had gone terribly wrong the past few days, she was getting screwed on her commission. Bird glared at Vicky: Final note to self: Slash the tires on that chiseler's chair.

Under the bounty hunter's intense glare, Vicky suddenly found her own fingernails very interesting and set about examining them more closely.

"Maybe," Dippo said in his slow, deliberate way, "maybe he got lost somewhere. He's not the brightest hammer in the bunch. We may still have a shot at finding him before he delivers Billy."

Bird turned to her troublesome partner. "Jesse, your stupid plan . . . ," and just like that, Bird's intense frown blossomed into a smile, "just might work! OK, we have to track down Mochabean fast. I figure we split up and start at the titty bars, then we work our way to the—"

"No need. I know exactly where to find him, man," Jesse interjected.

Slowly, all eyes turned to the pacifist yoga practitioner. Everyone was quite taken aback. Jesse knew exactly where to find Mochabean. Who had Billy. Whom they needed to trade for

Ruby. Jesse, the goober who not more than five minutes ago was standing on his head against the wall, had just saved the day.

"Not so useless now, am I?" he beamed.

•

Jesse parked across the street from a restaurant with the neon words BANANA CABANA blazing over the front door. Mochabean's truck sat out front.

"There's his truck, man, just like I said." Jesse squinted at the pickup. "See how the front grill is all messed up? That's from ramming it into my baby's rear bumper. Big, stupid cue ball."

"Well, I'll be." Bird was starting to see Jesse in a whole new light. First he saved her from getting mauled by that supposed dog, and now he'd brought her directly to Mochabean. Maybe Jesse wasn't a complete waste of brain cells after all. "OK, I give. How could you possibly know he'd be here?"

"They use organically grown fruit in their drinks." He smiled, as if that was all the explanation required.

After it became clear he wasn't going to continue, Bird could feel her constant companion, Irritation, building up in her. His good friend, Cold Rage, was bringing up the rear. "And?" she said, trying to mask her annoyance.

"That's why I come here all the time. And I always see Mochabean in here after he snags a skip. He likes to order this huge drink called the Coco Loco."

"Coco Loco?"

"Yeah," Jesse continued, "he forces the perps to have drinks with him before he turns them in."

"Why?" she asked, still not sure if there was any logic to what Jesse was saying.

"I think it's the only way he can get anyone to spend time

with him—in handcuffs. Not exactly the life of the party, that Mochabean."

Bird looked at the old truck with the broken front grill. She also noticed the driver's side door had a large dent, probably from smashing it into Billy when he was running past. In fact, the pickup was full of dents and scratches. Was each one of those the result of Mochabean's violent nature? Yeah, she wouldn't want to spend any time with the guy either if she had any choice in the matter. Still, part of her couldn't help but feel a little sad for a guy who had to handcuff people in order to have a little human companionship.

"OK, I'm going in. You wait here."

"I can help, man," Jesse said as he unbuckled his seat belt.

Bird clicked the belt back on him. "Jesse, I'm about to confront one of the meanest sons of bitches I've ever had the misfortune to run across. On top of that, he feels I owe him a great deal of money. I could use a lot of things right now. A pacifist is not one of them."

"Are you sure? I could—"

"I'm sure," she cut him off. Bird held up Big Bertha, which she'd borrowed from Vicky before leaving the office. Sometime in the past week, between the animal attacks and the Mob attacks and the high-speed wheelchair chase, she'd managed to misplace her own gun. It wasn't such a big loss—indeed, it was just a Chinese knockoff—but if she was going up against Mochabean again, she'd need some serious weaponry. And she was all out of baseball bats.

Jesse looked downcast, but he knew better than to press Bird on something once she'd made up her mind. Besides, how can you argue with someone holding that hefty hand cannon?

"Keep the engine running. And keep your eye on that front door." She pointed at the restaurant. "Be ready to go the second you see me come out. You can't miss me—I'll be the one running for her life."

As Bird walked toward the Banana Cabana, she rubbed the gun hidden in her pocket for reassurance. The last time she'd fired a weapon was when she'd tried to shoot out the Lincoln's tire to rescue her sister, and that didn't exactly go according to plan.

It's not that she had delusions of a peaceful coexistence with enemies and of talking out problems instead of resorting to violence. As far as she was concerned, Jesse and his pacifist ways were in the same camp as people who used to believe the earth was flat: a reasonable idea at first glance, but ultimately sheer and utter folly resulting from a fundamental lack of information. If there's one thing Bird had learned from her time on the police force, it was that no matter how willing you are to peacefully resolve a confrontation, some jack-off is just as willing to stick a Glock in your face, or a knife in your gut, or a needle in your neck, and so on and so forth, until you finally wise up and learn to protect yourself. That said, she still didn't want to be responsible for ending another human being's life, no matter how much they deserved to be put down. It just wasn't in her nature.

Still, Bird knew she'd put a bullet in Mochabean if it was the difference between life and death for her sister, Ruby. And, let's face it, that's exactly what it was. She gripped Big Bertha tightly and thought about nonlethal spots she could shoot Mochabean if it came to it: an arm, a leg, perhaps a foot if her aim was good enough. Stay away from the trunk of the body; it's full of vital organs. And definitely not the head, though, who knows, Mochabean had such a dense cranium, the bullet might just bounce off. At any rate, he'd better not even think of crossing swords with her, because Ladybird Blacker was through getting pushed around by everyone. No more games. Her sister's life was at stake, and no one, not even Mochabean, was going to stand in her way.

She held up Big Bertha in her right hand, its metallic heft strengthening her resolve. Bird stood at the front door of the Banana Cabana, and she could hear raucous laughter from inside. She'd probably have to break a few laws when she set foot in there, but laws be damned. Feeling she could storm the gates of hell itself, she set her jaw and kicked the door in, a lethal dose of lead poisoning ready for any fool who got in her way.

That's when she saw the place was full of cops. There were at least a half dozen of them, with four LAPD officers sitting in a booth by the front door. They were laughing, enjoying themselves, and as such did not immediately turn to see who had slammed open the door. This gave Bird, whose jaw had gone from resolute to dragging on the floor, the split second she needed to dive back outside. When an officer did turn, all he saw was an empty doorway.

Outside, Bird pressed against the wall, hyperventilating. "Shit!" she wheezed. "Shit, shit, shit!" She had almost marched in waving around a mini-Howitzer in a cop bar! Why had Jesse neglected to mention that small detail? "You idiot," she hissed at Jesse across the street. "It's full of cops in there!"

Meanwhile, Jesse was too far away to hear what she was saying and only saw her waving her arms around vigorously. He waved back and gave her a thumbs-up.

Well, so much for storming the gates of hell. If anyone in there saw Big Bertha, Bird would have a lot of explaining to do. And forget about getting Billy away from Mochabean then; they'd be long gone. This would require finesse. Time for plan B.

She shoved the overgrown gun into the waist of her pants and covered it with her jacket, but even concealed it bulged grotesquely under her clothes. And it was so heavy it was pulling down her pants. She'd have to leave it out here. A quick search revealed a nearby potted plant where Bird stashed the bulky weapon. "Sorry, Bertha, much as I would have liked to bring you along, you have to sit this one out."

This time when Bird walked into the Banana Cabana, one of the uniformed cops looked her up and down, taking in every detail. "Evening, officer," Bird said as she walked past.

Satisfied all was in order, the policeman nodded, said, "Ma'am," and turned back to his colleagues.

Even when she was on the force, Bird was never much for mingling with coworkers, but she had to admit she felt a pang at seeing the group of cops and the friendly camaraderie they shared. It was one of the things she missed most from the old days: she knew there was a group of people who had her back, a family she could always count on. At least, until she royally screwed everything up by screwing her partner's wife. Then that "family" had turned on her so fast you'd have thought they were just looking for an excuse to do so.

Ah, well, that was ancient, ugly history. She had plenty of current, even uglier, matters to deal with, and she saw one of them now, sitting in a back booth. Three Band-Aids were plastered on the side of Mochabean's bald head where she had cracked him with the baseball bat. Across from the giant bounty hunter, Billy Veach hunched down in the booth, doing his best to turn invisible.

Bird decided to keep her distance for the time being and play it by ear. She sat one booth down, behind Mochabean, where the booth wall was tall enough to keep him from noticing her but not so tall that she couldn't hear what they were saying. She caught Mochabean in the middle of a rather disturbing story.

"That was the first time I ripped a guy's arm outta its socket, but not the last," the bald man said with surprisingly little emotion. "So, whadda you think about my name? Mochabean—kinda strange name for a kid to grow up with, isn't it?"

"I love it!" Billy blurted out as he cowered in the booth seat. "I love your name. I think it's great. Very unique."

Mochabean squinted at him suspiciously. He tried to find some truth in Billy's eyes. But all he could see at the moment was fear.

"Ah, you're just saying that 'cause you're scared of me." He swigged the last of the Coco Loco, his preferred drink, then looked at the empty coconut shell. Billy gulped loudly, though he wasn't drinking anything.

"Everyone's scared of me . . . " Mochabean's words trailed off. Was that a hint of sadness in his voice? Whatever it was, it quickly disappeared behind his permanent scowl. "Well, they should be. I am a scary guy."

Billy had no clue what to say, as more than anything he wanted to keep his arms in their sockets. "I—I don't . . . ," he stammered.

Mochabean rose to his full height, towering over Billy, who looked on fearfully. The big man stretched his back with a crack loud enough to signify vertebral damage in average human beings. Then the giant cracked his knuckles—Pop! Snap! Crack! A timid whimper escaped Billy's trembling lips.

"I gotta take a leak," Mochabean said, gazing down at Billy Veach. "When I get back, remind me to tell you about the time I took a bullet in the head."

Bird covered her face with a menu as the big man lumbered past toward the john. She had to make her move now; she might not get another chance.

"What—what is that guy?" a scared Billy asked the heavens.

Just then, Bird slipped into the empty seat across from Billy. "I hear the drinks are good here."

"Oh, thank God it's you. Please, get me the fuck away from him." Billy looked around nervously, expecting an enormous shadow to befall them at any second.

Funny, this is the first bail jumper who's ever been glad to see me, Bird thought wryly. That gorilla must have done quite a number on this poor bastard. Even other pros in the fugitive-recovery business shiver at the thought of having a run-in with Mochabean. She could only imagine what kind of hell the poor skips he caught went through.

She grabbed Billy's arm and said, "Let's go." She tried to drag him off, but Billy yanked her back. The man's right wrist was handcuffed under the table to one of the metallic table legs, which was bolted to the ground. He wasn't going anywhere without a blowtorch. Or a key.

"No worries." Bird searched through her jacket pocket. She pulled out a small leather satchel.

"What's that?" Billy asked.

"I'm always prepared." She took out a ring of keys from the satchel and jingled them. "I should have something here that works."

She worked through the keys, trying each one on the handcuffs.

"Hurry." Nervous sweat beaded on Billy's brow. "I think maybe the guy's crazy. Like certifiably, you know?"

"Mochabean? Oh, yeah, he's a total psychopath."

"The stuff he told me, the things he's done, I've never heard anything like that." Billy grabbed Bird's arm. "And my father's a crime boss!"

Bird turned a key in the cuffs. "Ah, here we go. Sixth time's the charm." She opened the handcuffs and smiled.

The smile vanished as soon as she looked up.

All the blood had drained from Billy's face. He was ash white and staring wide-eyed at a spot approximately six feet and seven inches above Bird. She didn't need to look back—she knew who was there—but hope springs eternal, and so she slowly turned and hoped to God a certain bald giant was not there waiting for her.

"If it isn't my old pal, Bird Blacker." Mochabean grinned like a kid who'd just gotten exactly what he wanted for Christmas. "You must have a death wish trying to steal another skip from me."

"Mochabean. Just let me explain, OK?" Bird held up her hands defensively and gave as friendly a smile as she could muster.

Two enormous hands dropped onto her shoulders. She grimaced in pain as they squeezed like hydraulic clamps, crushing the life out of her.

Now free from the handcuffs, and perhaps hoping no one would notice him in the commotion, Billy took the opportunity to try to sneak out of the booth.

Without even turning to him, Mochabean said coldly to Billy, "Go ahead. Make me angrier."

"I wasn't, I was only . . . " Billy quickly scuttled back into the booth seat where he sat and awaited his fate.

Meanwhile, Bird was about a hair's breadth from passing out, the ogre's hands mashing down on her. She reached for her gun, then remembered she'd left it in the potted plant outside because of the . . . cops! She looked over at the laughing policemen. Amazingly, not one had noticed the slow-motion murder taking place a few feet away from them.

Mochabean saw she was about to call for help. "What, them? You think I'm scared of them?" He nodded toward the officers.

"Go ahead and call them. The more the merrier." And those rough hands squeezed even harder on her upper torso.

Bird grunted in agony, and her legs crumbled under her. She didn't fall to the ground, however, because even as Mochabean crushed her, he held her aloft in his grip. Even if she wanted to call out to the cops, she no longer had the breath to do so; they'd never hear her cries.

She had to act fast. Her vision was tunneling, and in a few seconds she'd surely lose consciousness. Mustering what little strength remained in her broken body, she murmured, "Not here for Billy . . . " She gasped and her eyes rolled back. "Here for you."

"You don't say. And whadda you want with me? A friendly game of baseball, maybe?" Mildly intrigued, he relieved a bit of the pressure on her shoulders.

In the booth, Billy was curled up in the fetal position with his hands over his face. "Oh, God, oh, God," he whimpered over and over.

After a few seconds, Bird managed to suck in enough air to utter a few more words. "Have business proposition . . . for you."

Mochabean lifted her up to eye level, her feet dangling underneath. It was the second time in a week that Mochabean had given a Blacker sister the rag-doll treatment. Bird hoped it didn't become a habit for the man.

"Let me guess. You pay me not to snap you in half?" He shook her once easily to demonstrate that he could, whenever and wherever, even in a roomful of LAPD officers.

Bird's head wobbled around like one of those ubiquitous bobble figures you see on car dashboards. But at least she could breathe again. "I want you to join me . . . for a job." She didn't exactly know where she was going with this, but he reduced a bit more of the strain on her shoulders, so she decided to keep running with it.

"You want to work with me?" He lowered her to the floor and stopped squeezing, though he kept holding her. Good thing too, since she'd probably collapse otherwise.

The tingling in her extremities meant blood was once again pumping through Bird's arms. She felt like a boulder had been lifted from her shoulders. If she kept working this angle, she might still make it out of the Banana Cabana without requiring major surgery.

"Why would Bird Blacker want to work with me?" He sounded suspicious, though he couldn't hide a sliver of pleasure in his voice. Bird was onto something.

"I have a very important job going down." In the few seconds it took Mochabean to lower her to the floor instead of pulverizing her, Bird had formulated a plan. With no trace of irony, she said, "I need you to back me up."

"What about your hippie? What's his name—Jesse?"

"I don't think my hippie's up for it. This is really big. Life-and-death big."

Mochabean considered this for a few seconds; meanwhile, Bird hoped to God he'd bought the routine. And since her life had already flashed before her eyes while he was crushing her, she took this time to go over only the highlights: a mother from hell, a crappy job, a horrendous love life, and a sister kidnapped by a crime lord. If her luck held true, not only would Mochabean not believe her, he'd also snap her neck. At least then she'd be out of her misery.

Amazingly, though, it seemed Mochabean did believe she'd come to the lovely Banana Cabana for him and not Billy. "Yeah," he said finally, "I wouldn't put my life in his hands either."

"I need someone with your experience, with your

obvious . . . talents." She stroked his ego like a horny teenager on prom night. To her great surprise, it worked.

Mochabean removed his meaty hands from her shoulders. She wasn't ready, though, and almost crumpled to the floor. She put a trembling hand against the table to help steady herself as her legs slowly came back to life.

"So, we'd work together? Like a team?" Something had changed in Mochabean—he was still big and scary, but he was no longer radiating waves of pure, concentrated fury. While Bird still feared that the Goliath would kill her, she no longer felt he would do so in a particularly grizzly manner.

"That's the deal." Bird rubbed gently at her aching shoulders. "Unless, of course, you got better things to do." She held up the shell of the Coco Loco Mochabean had been sipping.

Mochabean looked down at the empty drink. The coconut's once-white flesh had turned brown, and a tiny umbrella sticking out of the top was more sad than festive. It was Mochabean's lonely life in a tropical shell. "You know, you try anything clever, and I'll twist your head off," he warned.

"See, that's what I like about you." Bird smiled. "You don't let anyone mess with your head." She chuckled, taking secret pleasure in her clever manipulation of the big ox. But she immediately felt a stabbing pain in her torso, like one of her lungs had burst, and figured maybe she hadn't been all that clever after all.

"What the hell—this might be distracting." Mochabean took the tiny umbrella from his Coco Loco and picked his teeth with it, the colorful top sticking out of his mouth. "So, what's this big bugaboo you can't do without me?"

Bird hesitated before answering. Might as well lay it all out for him—who knows, it may even scare him off, and he would be out of her hair. "We're going to rescue my sister from the city's biggest criminal organization," she said flatly.

Mochabean chewed on his little umbrella, then answered, "Yeah, OK."

•

Moments later in the parked van, Jesse was startled when the side door slid open to reveal Mochabean standing there, big as life and looking right at him.

"Oh, shit!" Jesse cried out, no doubt expecting another beating from the man.

But to Jesse's great surprise, Mochabean stepped into the van, said, "Hey, partner," and made himself comfortable in back. He stretched out, taking full advantage of the fact that the vehicle had no rear seats to cramp his long legs.

Bird shoved Billy Veach, who remained cuffed, into the van and took her seat.

Jesse stared at her questioningly and nodded at Mochabean. "What's he doing here?" he whispered.

"Just play along," she whispered back. "He's with us."

"He's dangerous." Jesse mimed strangling himself, recalling how Mochabean had tried to choke him.

"I know." She rubbed her shoulders gently and tried not to breathe too deep, as it still hurt her lungs. "Believe me, I had no choice." She looked back at Mochabean.

"We gonna do this, or what?" the scowling bounty hunter said.

"The meet isn't for a few hours," said Bird. "You know, this looks like a shifty neighborhood. Maybe you want to take your truck and meet us there . . . ?"

"No." He placed one immense hand on Billy's head, like he was a favorite pet that could run off at any moment into the middle of traffic.

"Fine, whatever you prefer," Bird said, then turned away and mumbled through gritted teeth, "Shit."

Billy Veach tried to move the hand from his head, to no avail—Mochabean's grip was as tight as a vise and not easily escaped. As Bird, Ruby, and Jesse had all recently learned. It took a force of nature, or several whacks to the skull with a baseball bat that then shatters to splinters, to get him to release.

"Stop squirming," Mochabean said, and gave a squeeze that made Billy go cross-eyed.

"Ow," Billy protested, then called out to Bird, "Hey, what exactly are you going to do with me?"

"We're going to see Daddy," she said.

13

LOVE AND BAIT

ON ITS BEST DAY Da Vinci Bail Bonds wouldn't win any design awards, but at the moment it looked like a hurricane had blasted in through the front door, had its way with the place, and then left out the back. Although Dippo had cleaned up some, there was only so much he could do with bullet holes and smashed windows.

The mild-mannered assistant now sat quietly at his desk and worked in the silent office. He looked up and found Vicky leafing halfheartedly through a manila folder, no doubt some other miscreant she'd bonded who would likely lead to hassle and ruin for them all. That was the crux of the problem: they were in the business of dealing with the shadier elements—in fact, of facilitating the exit of criminals from jail, if only till their court date came up. Was it any surprise then that many of their "clients," far from being grateful for the service Da Vinci Bail Bonds provided, instead skipped out and ran as far and as fast as possible to ensure they never had to deal with a judge, Vicky, or any bounty hunters she may send after them? Sure, there was the whole innocent-till-proven-guilty spiel, and many of the people Vicky provided bond for did follow their civic duty and show up for court, but far too many others were no-good criminals, plain and simple. Which only made it surprising that the office didn't get shot up more often.

"Do you suppose . . . ," Dippo asked of Vicky, "do you suppose they'll make it through this? Unharmed, I mean."

Vicky didn't look away from her file. "Bird will figure something out."

"But will they be OK?" Dippo insisted.

Vicky sighed loudly and looked around the wrecked office. "Look, the shit already hit the fan, OK? I hope they'll be all right, but this is the life we lead."

"Yes, you never know what'll happen these days . . . " He opened his mouth to continue, but chickened out at the last moment. Instead, he looked down at the paperwork on his desk. He took a deep breath, mustering his courage, and closed his eyes.

Finally, Dippo blurted out, "Would you like to go out with me?"

Vicky was somewhat taken aback, to say the least. Always one with a snappy retort, she was unprepared for such a question from her meek office assistant. Her mouth stayed open for a few seconds until words finally found their way out. "I—I beg your pardon?" she said, uncertain.

But if Vicky was for once having difficulty finding words, then Dippo found himself in just as unlikely a position, with words now flooding out of him rapid-fire. "I just meant to get coffee that's all not something inappropriate or anything like that I'm going for coffee you see do you want anything no you don't drink coffee do you no coffee for you then maybe tea or not OK good-bye." In his nervous state he'd lumped all his thoughts into one long run-on sentence. And the longer Vicky remained silent and stared at him, the worse his chattering became, until the only option left for Dippo was a hasty escape.

He backed out the front door and stumbled over the broken frame on his way out. Meanwhile, Vicky looked on in confusion as her normally dependable, not-at-all-chatty assistant practically tap-danced as he exited stage left.

After he left, Vicky furrowed her brow in concentration as she tried to puzzle out what had just occurred. Maybe he'd been struck on the head during the office raid. Maybe the pressures of the job were finally getting to him. Before she could formulate a hypothesis, she saw Dippo stride back in, a determined look on his face.

"A date. With me. And you." He made sure to pause after each phrase—no more of that nervous chatter for him. "Us together. Datewise." Having said this, he shut his eyes tight, as if expecting a punch to the face.

When Vicky answered, "O-OK," Dippo opened one eye hopefully, and said, "Yeah?"

Vicky looked down at her wheelchair, battered and bent from bouncing down the street after they'd rescued her. One wheel was now bent at an angle, and the other barely hung on. One armrest had the bullet hole from Bird's errant shot, and the other rest was missing completely. But even if it had been a shiny new wheelchair, fresh off the assembly line in China, or wherever it is they made the awful things, it would still be a wheelchair. Even if it was in perfect working order . . . she never would be.

Vicky was a strong woman, some would even refer to her as a tough broad, but even she could not disguise the quiver in her voice as she asked, "Are you quite certain this is what you want?" She gripped tightly the remaining armrest for support. She'd given him a way out and waited for him to take it. Instead, it was a pleasant surprise when he gently placed his hand over hers on the armrest and gave it a squeeze.

"Yes, quite certain," he said, smiling warmly as he looked down.

They remained so until the moment almost became awkward, but just before it did, a mischievous smile grew on Vicky's face. "I like lobster," she said with a toothy grin.

"Lucky me," Dippo responded wryly.

Just then Ruby ran through the open front door. She was breathing hard and covered in sweat. Vicky and Dippo instantly flew apart from each other, like a couple of nervous teens who'd just been caught making out behind the school bleachers.

"Ruby? How marvelous," Vicky said, a little too giddy. "Look, Dippo, it's Ruby."

"Yes, I can see that," he said, just as giddy.

Vicky wobbled in her chair over to Ruby and hugged the girl like she was family. "I am so glad to see you."

"Thanks," Ruby said, still catching her breath. "Where's Bird?"

"Isn't she with you?" Vicky looked at the girl confused.

"Uh, no. I just spent half the night looking for a taxi. Man, this whole city shuts down after 2:00 A.M." She dropped into the nearest chair to rest.

Vicky noticed the stains on Ruby's pants. "Is that—oh, my God—is that blood? Are you all right?"

"Blood?" She looked down at her legs. "Oh, that. Don't worry about it."

"That's not your blood?" Dippo asked.

Ruby tongued her sore cheeks. "No, it's my blood all right. I wouldn't be here without it. So where's Bird? She'll never believe how I escaped."

"My dear, Bird and Jesse set off to rescue you hours ago." Vicky exchanged a worried look with Dippo.

"Rescue me? They did that, really?" She smiled, evidently pleased at the idea that they thought so highly of her. Imagine that, a rescue party for little her. She couldn't even get a jump start the last time her car battery died.

"They went to a warehouse to trade Billy Veach for you," Dippo chimed in.

Ruby's smile suddenly froze in horror as she realized what would likely happen when her sister showed up at the warehouse. Bird would encounter a roomful of criminals awfully cranky over the fact that their hostage had escaped and roughed up one of their men.

"Oh, no."

14

SIMPLE PLANS
AND SIMPLE MEN

THE FIRST THING THE enforcer saw when she strode into the festive Party Palace warehouse was Mr. V's trusted bodyguard sitting tied to a chair. Goldie looked like he'd gone twelve rounds with a cement wall. She noticed, in fact, that his telltale gold tooth was no longer in his mouth, which was cut and bleeding. She picked up the shiny tooth off the ground near him.

"Missing something?" She held up his sparkly tooth between two fingers. "You don't look so tough now, do you?"

"Neither do you, bitch," he said, referring to the big, black shiner on her left eye. Apparently, she had gone a few rounds herself.

She raised her fist to do a little more dental work on Goldie, when a voice stopped her cold.

"Stop that!" Mr. V jogged into the room, his second bodyguard at his side.

She flinched and reflexively brought a protective hand up to her black eye.

"And this, what's this?" Mr. V nodded at the incapacitated bodyguard.

"I loosened her ropes just for a second." The fear in Goldie's voice was unmistakable. No matter what kind of beating he'd taken from Ruby, it paled in comparison to what Billy Veach could do to him.

"You gotta understand, she ain't normal," he said desperately. " She went apeshit on me. She was too fast—feet and fists flying everywhere like some kinda whirlwind. Jesus, I think she broke my arm." Goldie's right hand was turned back, the wrist at an unnatural angle. Even if the arm hadn't been tied down, it would have been useless to the big man.

"Strange, I had no trouble handling the teenage girl." The enforcer smirked.

"You mean to tell me, one little girl did this?" Mr. V reached down and squeezed the bodyguard's mangled arm. The man howled in pain and writhed under the ropes. "To you, my own personal bodyguard, who is supposed to be keeping me safe?"

"Nice going, kid," the woman mumbled appreciatively.

"She must have been quite the athlete," the crime boss said. "I bet she had superb muscle tone. Did you happen to notice?"

Goldie was sweating bullets by the boxful now. He'd seen this before; he knew where Mr. V was likely going with the nonchalant attitude and the questions that didn't seem to have anything to do with the situation at hand.

"I'm still not at my peak heart rate." Mr. V checked his pulse rate and wiped his brow with a small towel. Then he looked over at Goldie. "Well, did she?" he asked.

"I'll get her back, sir, I swear I will," Goldie blurted, his brow damp from pain and fear.

The crime lord shook his head in disappointment; he was an oh-so-wise teacher who just could not get through to an especially dense student. "That's very kind of you. But—and stay with me here, because there's a twist—do you suppose you could get me Billy instead? You see, he's the one I actually wanted. The girl, well, she was just bait."

The enforcer chuckled. She was loving every excruciating detail of Goldie's suffering.

"Yeah, of course, Mr. V, of course." Perhaps it was simply the profuse sweating, but it looked an awful lot like he'd just wet his pants. "That's what I meant, sir. I'll get you Billy."

William Veach bent forward till he was face-to-face with the sitting bodyguard. He pointed at his nose and smiled innocently. "I seem to have an itch on the tip of my nose."

"An itch?" Goldie said with genuine confusion.

"Yes, right there on the tip." He wiggled his nose once.

"Um, sir? You want me to scratch your nose?"

"Would you mind?"

"No, of course not." He smiled nervously.

But of course Goldie was still tied down and couldn't scratch even his own nose, let alone anyone else's. He waited for someone to untie him. But no one moved to help. Panicking, Goldie pulled and strained at his bonds, twisting pathetically in the chair. Under different circumstances maybe, just maybe, the brawny bodyguard would have been able to break free, but with a broken arm? Forget about it.

The enforcer laughed openly now. Finally, Goldie was getting his comeuppance for being a grade-A asshole, 100-percent free of any redeeming qualities. His squirming couldn't last long enough for her. She contained her mirth only when Mr. V shot her a disapproving gaze.

"Well?" he said, still peering into Goldie's eyes.

"I—I can't." The bodyguard slumped in the chair, finally accepting defeat.

"That's right. You can't." Mr. V rose to his full height and pointed an accusatory finger down at Goldie. "Because you let a goddamn teenage girl kick your ass and tie you to a goddamn chair, you useless lump of shit!"

The bodyguard wilted even further under his boss's assault, but there was nowhere he could hide. All he could do was sit and take it, his broken arm throbbing at his side.

Mr. V's second bodyguard shifted uncomfortably from foot to foot behind him. That was his partner, after all, getting reamed. Even the enforcer wasn't enjoying the show as much. Truth be told, she wasn't much for verbal abuse. For some reason she got considerably more pleasure from pummeling someone with her bare hands than from calling them names.

"And you're going to get me back my son?" The worked-up crime lord took his towel and whipped Goldie across the face. "You couldn't find a Catholic in Rome! I'm surrounded by incompetents. Everywhere I look I see failure." And with that, he made sure to lock eyes with his female enforcer and top assassin.

"I'm sorry, Dad—"

"Don't you call me that!" He thrust a quivering finger in her face, his own features a demonic mask of anger. "Understand this: Your mother was little more than a common whore. That I took pity on you, the unwanted fruit of our 'dealings,' does not make you family. It does not make you my blood. And it certainly does not make you my daughter!"

The words stabbed into her, through skin and flesh and bone, directly into her palpitating heart. For a few blindingly painful seconds she could neither breathe nor talk. Even blinking proved difficult as she stared into her father's cold eyes.

In all her years of "tying up" loose ends for his organization, she'd been on the receiving end of quite a bit of punishment. She'd been shot twice, once by police, once by a drug dealer; she'd broken a rib, her wrist, and her right leg; she'd even been impaled by a broken golf club that was millimeters from puncturing a vital organ. But nothing she'd been through could compare to the pain her father inflicted on her on a regular basis. Even the piercing, cold pain of a knife blade slicing into her gut would have been a thousand times preferable to this.

"Now pull yourself together and get me back my son." Mr. V walked away from the stunned woman.

"I . . . ," she squeezed out. Then she cast her gaze down in shame. "Yes, sir."

Mr. V, all the passion now drained from his voice, nodded at the tied-up bodyguard. "But first, break all his fingers."

"Sir?" she asked.

"One must punish failure, or it becomes acceptable behavior."

"Yes, sir," she said, emulating the coldness in her father's voice.

A short while later, when she dutifully set about following her father's orders, Goldie's screams reverberated throughout the warehouse.

•

"We're almost there," Jesse announced as he drove.

Bird had put on her bulletproof vest. She glumly stared down at the hole in the middle of it, a chunk still missing thanks to her run-in with a certain rambunctious canine. She sighed and took the thing off; it would be of little use now.

She began methodically checking each of her bullets, as was her way. Normally, the routine helped calm her, put her nerves at ease. It was having no such effect this time. Suddenly, it dawned on her what a monumental waste of time her idiosyncrasies were. Her little sister needed her, now, and she didn't have time to be dicking around counting bullets. Whatever went down that day, whatever she had to do to save Ruby, she knew it would not make a difference how symmetrical her bullets were, or how perfect the crease on her pants was, or—and she hated to admit this one—whether her hands were disinfected. In fact, if there's one thing she could be certain of, it was that things were about to get real messy.

To hell with it, maybe it would do her good to cut loose a little. She shoved the bullets into Big Bertha and chambered a round.

"OK, this is the place up ahead," Jesse said.

The Party Palace warehouse came into view. It looked like any other warehouse—large, boxlike, and otherwise nondescript, except for a neon-orange storefront on one side declaring a 50 percent–off sale on propane refills this week only. Evidently, when it came to flammable gas, William Veach passed the savings on to you.

"Don't park too close," Bird said. "I don't want them to know we're coming. Mochabean, you sneak around the back of the building and wait for my signal. Jesse, you're—"

"What's the signal?" Mochabean interrupted.

"I don't know, I'll whistle or something. Jesse, you—"

"What kind of whistle?" he insisted.

"Ooh, can I give the signal?" Jesse said excitedly.

"No, I will give the signal." Bird could feel the veins in her forehead begin to throb. "Jesse, you—"

"What kind of whistle?" Mochabean still wanted to know.

"Why can't I give the signal, man?" Jesse whined in an especially nasal manner.

"Because," Bird said, "I know for a fact you will mess it up."

"Jeez," Jesse snorted, "what's so hard about giving a signal, anyway?"

"What's the signal?" Mochabean's one-track mind would not get off that rail.

"The signal, man, the signal," Jesse said in a superior tone. "So you know to make your move. That's how teams work— with signals."

Mochabean squinted one eye and curled his lip. "I know what a signal is, you squirrel."

"All right, everyone shut up!" Bird had finally had enough. She felt the start of a migraine and could barely think straight with all the nonsense flying around her. "The signal will be a simple, loud whistle. That's it, nothing fancy. OK? All right? Can we drop it? Good . . . Now—"

"Come to think of it, I can't whistle anyway," Jesse cut in.

Bird whacked him on the back of the head.

"Ow!" Jesse rubbed at his skull.

"Now, then." Bird handcuffed herself to Billy. "You stick with me. Try anything in there, and I guarantee you are meat. Understand?"

"Whatever. I'm not the one you should be worried about."

"Oh? And who should I be worrying about?"

"My sister. She's a rabid dog."

"Who's your sister?" Bird said, only half listening as she continued to prepare for the upcoming meet.

"Kaya. She does 'jobs' for my father."

Bird suddenly froze. "Kaya . . . ?" The name trailed off on her lips. It couldn't possibly be the same woman. Not her Kaya. Not the Second Biggest Mistake of Her Life. There must be hundreds of Kayas in Los Angeles. Or at least dozens. Her luck couldn't possibly be that bad. Could it?

"She ties up loose ends." Billy word's brought her back to the moment. "Permanently. And she's probably coming after me next."

"What does this Kaya look like?" Bird asked.

"Big, ugly bitch," Billy spat out. "Dreadful as death itself."

Well, that settled that. Her Kaya was drop-dead beautiful; it's what drew Bird to her in the first place. His Kaya sounded, well, butch. Definitely not the same woman. Besides, Bird refused to accept that on top of everything else—a rabid hound almost eating her, her nosy sister getting kidnapped, Mochabean almost crushing her—she would also have to deal with her ex-girlfriend now trying to kill her. "I'll keep an eye out for her," she said, somewhat relieved.

"She's always riding my ass," Billy continued. "Just because I went to college instead of running around cracking heads like she did. Says I don't deserve the Veach name. That I'm not a real man . . . Fuck her!"

"This is your sister you're talking about?" She couldn't fathom how anyone could speak of family that way.

"Half sister," Billy said. "When she found out my father wants me—not her!—to take over the business . . . I honestly thought she was gonna kill me then and there. Fucking slag."

Bird looked at the crooked Polaroid on the van's dashboard—Ruby smiled brightly at her from the picture. No matter how much trouble Ruby could be, Bird would never speak of her own sister in such hateful terms. She ran a finger across it and straightened the picture.

"So, where do you want me, man?" Jesse said. "Covering the back, or in through the front?"

Bird shook her head. "Mochabean, you got the rear. Head around back and don't be seen." She slid open the door to let the big man out.

The giant nodded once, then snuck away toward the Party Palace. He looked like a tiptoeing buffalo, though he was quiet enough. If nothing else, at least he'd be out of her way.

Bird turned to her partner in fugitive recovery. "Jesse, you wait in the van. Keep it running. Same drill as last time."

He slapped the steering wheel. "Aw, man, again? When you gonna let me go in with you?"

Bird grabbed his shoulder. "Who's my getaway man? Who's the one guy I can always count on to pull my bacon out of the fire?"

Jesse pouted, looked away.

"Jesse?"

"I am, I guess," he answered, finally.

"That's right," Bird said with genuine earnest. "I've already got Mochabean to deal with in there. He's a total screwup. I need a pro out here, someone with your experience, to pull all our asses out of the deep fryer. Can I count on you? Are you my guy?" She looked him in the eye and held his gaze.

Jesse nodded. Yeah, he was her guy.

Bird tousled his hair. "Good. And don't let anyone sneak up on you out here."

"No one ever does, man," he assured her.

Bird shoved Billy Veach out the van.

"Hey," Jesse called out. "Out of curiosity, how much you paying Mochabean to help us out here?"

Bird thought about it. "Oddly enough, it never came up." She yanked the wrist cuffed to Billy. "Let's go, you."

•

When they were walking in the mostly vacant parking lot for the Party Palace warehouse, and out of earshot of anyone else, the accountant kept staring at Bird with a cockeyed grin.

"What?" she said.

"You're good."

Bird looked at him sideways. "It's a little late in the game to be coming on to me. Besides, you're not my type."

"No, I mean with people. Shifting them your way, to your advantage."

"Don't know what you're talking about." But, of course, she knew exactly what he was talking about. Though at first glance she might be considered the strong, silent type, Ladybird Blacker was actually quite skilled with words. Had been for as long as she could remember. Her mother used to say it didn't come from her side of the family—they liked to use many words to say as little as possible. So it must come from her father, this ability to charm people with a minimum amount of effort.

It's probably how I was conceived in the first place, she thought with a grin. So she could add manipulating people to the short list of things she inherited from her deadbeat father. Cheers, Da', she thought, and picked up the pace as she yanked at the cuffs that linked her to Billy.

When the pair reached the store side entrance, Bird knocked on the door. No one answered immediately, and she feared perhaps it was the wrong location, that she'd misheard the ransom directions. Wouldn't that be quite the screwup? But before the cold sweats kicked in, someone came to the entrance and unlocked the door for them.

He was a smiling middle-aged man in a cheap suit. Bird deduced he was the Party Palace store manager from the name tag he wore, which read: "Chad, Store Manager." Good to know she could have made detective after all.

"Hello! Welcome to the Party Palace," Chad said in a well-rehearsed salesman voice. "We're the county's most fully stocked party and picnic emporium. We carry everything from authentic Mexican piñatas to genuine Chinese fireworks."

"I'm here about Billy," Bird said, unmoved by his too perky tone. She raised a handcuffed hand.

The manager's smile disappeared instantly. No need to sell them on anything. "Oh. Come in then."

•

As they walked through the storefront, Bird examined the colorful merchandise. She'd never seen so many colors, candies, and party favors in one place; it looked like a clown had thrown up in there. "Jolly place you got here. Not at all what I was expecting, given the situation," she said. "Figured the place would be more . . . ominous, for some reason."

Chad the manager looked back at them and shook his head morosely, the salesman completely gone from his personality. "I don't know what business you have with Mr. V, and I don't want to know," he snapped. So much for the Blacker family charm. "Just go all the way down that hall and leave me out of it." He pointed down a corridor that led farther into the warehouse.

Bird and Billy made their way down the two hundred–foot hallway as the manager waved them on. He walked back to the storefront, grumbling about the rising cost of imported piñatas and how much cheaper the traditional Mexican items would be if he could import them from China.

"The shit I get into for family," Bird said to herself.

"Tell me about it," Billy agreed.

15

THE CAVALRY, THE RESCUE, AND VICE VERSA

DEAD CENTER IN THE main warehouse area, Goldie the bodyguard, who no longer had his gold tooth, had passed out from the pain of having all his fingers shattered. He slumped in the chair Ruby had secured him to during her escape.

Mr. V, meanwhile, was busy pumping out stomach crunches on the floor as his second bodyguard stood vigilantly by his side.

Nearby, Kaya the enforcer stroked her black eye. She looked over at her father and winced, maybe from the memory of him battering her face, or perhaps from the words that bruised her even worse. "Dad . . . " She hesitated. "Mr. V, I just want to say how sorry I am about all this."

Her father ignored her, concentrating on doing his crunches just right. Form is everything when it comes to getting results from exercise. Most people don't realize that.

Kaya continued, "Sir, all I've ever wanted was to earn your—"

"Not now, Kaya," he cut her off brusquely. "My ab regimen."

And then, in the middle of her pain and the crime boss's ab regimen, Bird Blacker quietly walked into the warehouse.

For the longest time she stared at Kaya.

Her Kaya.

The woman she had shared a bed and, for a short while, her life with. What were the odds? Easily a million to one. But, of course, it could be no other way, and somewhere she heard a cosmic rim shot indicating that she was, indeed, God's little punch line. "Where's my sister?" Bird finally managed to say.

Instantly, Kaya pulled her gun and had it aimed dead center at the intruder. A hint of a smile crossed her face as she recognized Bird.

The second bodyguard was noticeably slower in his reaction. Nonetheless, it was just as uncomfortable when he aimed his gun at Bird.

Mr. V, meanwhile, was almost finished with his set, and not about to let anyone interrupt him. "Sixty-eight," he grunted, "sixty-nine . . . and seventy." He jumped to his feet and looked over at Bird. "I'm sorry, you are . . . ?"

Before she could answer, Billy walked out from behind Bird.

"Billy, my boy!" the crime boss called out.

"Dad." The younger Veach moved toward his father, forgetting he was still attached to the bounty hunter.

She yanked him back to remind him. "You have my sister," Bird reminded them. "I want her back."

"Your sister . . . " For a second, Mr. V was thrown off. He looked over at Goldie, tied up in the chair and responsible for the young girl's escape. Bird had just given away that she wasn't up to speed on the latest events of the day.

"Yes, of course, your sister," he said with a friendly smile, as he stepped in front of the unconscious Goldie to block him from view. "But first, please let my son go."

"No. My sister first. Where's Ruby?"

"No, Ms. Blacker, first we meet my needs. As you can see,

the balance of power is somewhat tilted." He gestured at Kaya and the second bodyguard, both of whom had guns trained on Bird.

"You shoot me, I shoot Billy—we all lose." She shoved Big Bertha, the handgun on steroids, into Billy's gut, making him grunt in discomfort.

Kaya aimed her own weapon true. Her gaze was cold and held no indication that she wouldn't shoot her former lover. Despite trying to hide it, Bird couldn't help but tremble as a shiver ran down her spine. Her Kaya. Aiming a gun at her heart. Jesus, could this get any more symbolic? Once again, cue the cosmic rim shot.

She didn't recognize the other man—probably some goombah bodyguard. He was also aiming a gun at her. At the moment, that was the only thing about him that interested Bird.

Mr. V snapped his fingers. Without taking his eyes off Bird, the bodyguard pulled a clean towel from a duffel bag he carried around his shoulder and handed it to his boss, who wiped his face with it. "Forgive my appearance," said Veach. "I'm under a strict regimen of exercise and a fat-free diet. Would you believe I've had three heart attacks in the past two years?"

"That's the life of crime for you," Bird said dryly. "Leads straight to the grave."

The man was taken aback for the second time by the bounty hunter. He wasn't used to anyone speaking to him with such insolence. He kept his cool as he continued. "Possibly. Though I suspect my love of rich foods had more to do with it."

"Fascinating." Bird had no patience for chitchat, especially from the sweaty son of a bitch responsible for kidnapping her baby sister. Besides, she knew he was stalling. She figured something wasn't kosher the moment she walked in the door. "Let's get on with it already."

"Of course. You see, the bald truth of it, Ms. Blacker, is that I don't have your sister." Veach held out his empty palms.

"You lying turd. Ruby! Honey, where are you? Ruby!" she called out in the cavernous warehouse.

She'd had enough of this claptrap. Bird pointed her gun at Billy's temple, who shut his eyes tight and winced. "I want to see her now," Bird said, "or I blow his head clean off. I don't care if you shoot me."

The father held up his hands for her to stop. "Ms. Blacker— Bird—please calm down. No one here has to get hurt. I swear to you we don't have your sister."

"Don't worry, I can handle her, sir." Kaya closed one eye and took careful aim.

"Kaya, put the gun away."

She wet her lips. "Sir, just give me a chance. I swear to you I can do this."

"Woman, you are endangering the life of my son."

"He's in no danger from her," Kaya assured him. "She doesn't have the stomach for it."

William Veach reached over, snatched the gun from his bodyguard, turned, and aimed it at Kaya. "If you don't put down that gun this instant . . . "

"Mr. V—Dad," Kaya pleaded. "You wouldn't . . . "

For a long moment, Kaya scrutinized her father's face, perhaps looking for a trace of compassion in his eyes, for some sort of recognition that she was family and he would never shoot, that this was all a ploy to mislead the bounty hunter. But the only thing to be found in his eyes was cold resentment.

"Put it down. Now," he ordered. Then he cocked the gun,

and it was evident that he would kill her without hesitation to protect his son.

Kaya lowered her gun. A broken woman, she shambled away toward some forgotten corner of the warehouse where she could curl up and sink into darkness.

Bird, who had witnessed the exchange between father and daughter with a combination of disbelief and pity, thought to herself, Well, this explains a lot. Finally, her ex-girlfriend's violent nature and sadistic tendencies began to make some sense to her. It's no wonder she liked to hit people.

"There, see?" William Veach turned to Bird. "Now you have nothing to worry about. She's gone." Slowly, he lowered his gun to the floor.

"If you don't have my sister, where is she?"

He stepped aside and pointed at the unconscious bodyguard behind him. "She's such a clever girl, that sister of yours."

•

Still waiting in the van, Jesse concentrated on the doorway to the Party Palace. No one had come or gone since Bird had entered nearly half an hour ago. He knew because he hadn't so much as blinked the whole entire time. Now the dope's eyes were red and bloodshot.

"Nothing's getting past me. I'm a hawk. I'm an eagle. I'm, uh, I'm . . . " Jesse was so busy thinking of additional animals for his metaphor that he did not notice when a clown popped up right next to the driver's window.

"Hey, turkey," the jester said in a cheery voice.

"Ah, ah, clown!" Jesse nearly leaped out of his skin.

"Relax, Jesse, it's only me."

Jesse squinted suspiciously at the creature, with its orange

Afro wig, polka-dot pants, and floppy red shoes. Then he smiled as he recognized who was under the getup. "Marsha?" he said hopefully.

"No, you idiot. Ruby."

"Oh, ye-a-a-ah," Jesse exhaled. "See, I thought you were Marsha, my ex-girlfriend. She was into dressing up, costumes— you know, kinky stuff."

Ruby the clown rolled her eyes in that way only Blacker women could. "Where's Bird?"

Jesse nodded his head slightly as he fixed on Ruby's costume. He licked his lips lasciviously. Was he thinking back to the many fun times he had had with his kinky ex-girlfriend? "The things you can do with a red rubber nose . . . " His eyes glazed over.

"Jesse!"

"Huh, what? What's up, dude?" He was back, but couldn't help staring at Ruby's bright nose.

"My sister, where is she?"

"She's in there." Jesse pointed at the Party Palace warehouse a few hundred feet ahead of them. "Rescuing you . . . "

"That's what I was afraid of." The girl rubbed at her grease-painted chin pensively as she formulated a plan of attack. At times like these it was easy to tell she and Bird were related— they shared so many mannerisms. "That means I have to go in there and save her bacon after all. Look, if we're not out in twenty minutes, call the authorities."

Jesse hardly paid attention, mesmerized by the bulbous, shiny nose floating so close to him. "Yeah, I'll call the firemen."

"No, the cops, Jesse, call the cops."

"Yeah, man, whatever. That's what I meant."

"Are you . . . why are you staring at my nose like that?" Suddenly embarrassed, Ruby covered her face with her hand

and blushed. Her skin turned bright pink around her neck and wherever the thick white makeup didn't plaster her features.

Jesse coughed and shifted in his seat. "No reason. Right, I'll call the cops."

Ruby ran off toward the Party Palace warehouse, her big clown shoes flopping the whole way.

16

THE QUEEN OF KLOWN-FU

CHAD THE PARTY PALACE manager was back in salesman mode. He must have smelled a big sale the moment the clown walked in the door. Clowns are big business in the highly competitive party-supplies industry. "Welcome to the Party Palace," he said in his rehearsed voice. "We're the county's most fully stocked party and picnic—"

Ruby cut him off quickly. "I need piñatas—five hundred to start. The big, fat premium ones with the good chocolate inside. Not those little ones with the crappy candy corn."

Chad's greedy eyes nearly popped out of his skull—five hundred piñatas! This clown was definitely a high roller. "Oh, my! Yes, of course we can supply you. Please, follow me."

The grinning manager led Ruby down the same hallway that Bird had taken earlier. "Have I seen you in here before?" he said by way of chitchat.

"No," Ruby said hastily.

"You seem familiar. What's your name?"

"My name?" She looked around and saw a bag of fast food crumpled in a corner. "I'm Chili," she said in a high-pitched clown voice, "the, um, multicultural clown . . . Feliz navidad."

Chad bobbed his head up and down. "Chili, eh? I like it. The minority angle is big right now."

They turned and walked into a room halfway down the

hallway, well before reaching the main warehouse. Ruby glanced toward the end of the hall, down where she'd been held prisoner not long before.

"What's down there?" she asked innocently.

"That's off-limits. Some clients are conducting . . . a business transaction."

"Hey," she stopped suddenly and smiled. "Have you ever seen any of Bruce Lee's movies?"

The manager wrinkled his brow, confused by the non sequitur. "No, I don't think so. Why do you ask?"

"Dragon lashes out with his tail," she said, bending her knees slightly.

"Dragon does what now?" Poor Chad never saw the blow coming.

Lightning fast, Ruby twirled her body and whipped a devastating spin kick to the manager, her oversized shoe connecting with his chest in a loud Flomp! Chad went flying into the room and landed in a pile of piñatas, the colorful characters raining down on him.

"Sorry I had to do that," Ruby said. "Please be sensible and stay down."

There was no need to insist, however, since Chad was already unconscious, sprawled among the frilly, treat-filled piñatas.

Ruby closed the door to the storage room. She made her way silently back toward the main warehouse, where she had been held prisoner. She paused midsneak and cocked her head as a thought occurred to her. "Hey . . . I just invented klown-fu!" She gave a short snort of laughter, then continued down the hall.

Ruby tiptoed into the main warehouse area. She hid behind towering sacks of confetti stacked seven feet high. From there she could see her sister, Bird, and four other people in the center of the room, including the stupid guard she'd overpowered and tied to a chair. The warehouse was full of boxes, sacks, and containers, so Ruby had plenty of places to conceal herself. "OK, I'm in," she murmured. "Now what?"

In the center of the room, William Veach was still trying to convince an increasingly aggravated Bird to release his son, Billy. The crime lord's voice was slow and soothing to calm Bird and put her at ease. It was probably the friendliest tone he'd ever used in his adult life, but it was necessary since she was pointing an immense gun at his son's head.

"Let's work something out," he said softly. "All I want is my son safely back. Is that such an outrageous request? Your sister is probably safe back at home right now."

"How do I know you're not lying?" Bird squeezed the grip on Big Bertha and flexed her trigger finger.

"Think about it—why is my man sitting there unconscious? Why are his fingers broken? You don't think we did that to him, do you?"

When he heard that, the second bodyguard twitched uncomfortably, having witnessed the torturing of his friend firsthand. But he kept his mouth shut.

"Of course not," William Veach said sincerely. "Your sister did it when she escaped. I just want this over with. I just want my son back. I promise, let my boy go, and you walk out of here untouched. I give you my word as a father."

"She's safe . . . Ruby's safe." Bird sighed with relief. A boulder lifted off her back. Her baby sister was all right; she hadn't failed in her duty as an older sister.

"Yes, safe. Now, please . . . ," Veach continued in his thick, hypnotic voice, "let my son go."

Slowly, almost involuntarily, Bird lowered the gun from Billy's head. Something still nagged her, some niggling thought at the back of her mind, but it was nothing compared to the relief she felt at knowing her baby sister was no longer in danger. She opened the handcuffs and shoved Billy forward. "Go on."

"You weren't really going to shoot, were you?" Billy rubbed at the red marks on his wrist where the cuffs had bitten into his skin.

Bird did not look him in the eye, which was as good as a confirmation that, yes, she would have ventilated his head if it had come down to it. Thankfully, it had not come down to that, and her soul could remain a bit less besmirched.

The accountant walked to the crime lord, and for a fleeting moment, they were only father and son. A smiling William Veach wrapped his arms around Billy and kissed his forehead.

"Hey, Dad."

"You gave me quite the scare. Next time, you let me handle the legal matters. That way things won't get out of hand." William Veach tousled his son's hair, as he no doubt did when he was just a boy. You might think Billy Veach, a grown man for some time, would have outgrown such gestures. But evidently, this time he was willing to let it go. Billy smiled up at his tall father.

"Thank you, Ms. Blacker," Mr. V said to the bounty hunter. "Now, if you'll excuse me, I'm late for my cardiologist."

Bird nodded and walked toward the exit, when suddenly the second bodyguard grabbed his gun from the floor, where his boss had left it, and aimed the pistol at Bird, halting her in her tracks.

Oh, yeah, now she remembered what had been nagging her: these are criminals she's dealing with. And the only people who trust criminals are their mothers and bail bondsmen.

"Drop the gun," the bodyguard ordered. "Slowly. Then kick it over to me."

"Dad, what's going on?" Billy asked.

"Business as usual, that's what," said Bird.

"Please put your gun down, Ms. Blacker," William Veach said, the chill returning to his voice. "Obviously, I can't just let you walk out of here."

"Obviously," Bird said dryly. She kicked Big Bertha over, but she made sure to kick hard. Her gun slid past the bodyguard and crashed into a precariously stacked tower of boxes. The unbalanced tower fell apart, and boxes marked ACME Water Pistols crashed open, spilling dozens of realistic-looking toy guns. Finding Bird's weapon in that mess would be like, well, finding a gun in a pile of guns.

The bodyguard glared at her. He'd have to take his eyes off her to search for and retrieve Big Bertha. Bird just shrugged; nobody said she had to make it easy for him.

"Dad," Billy pleaded, "I don't want any part of this."

Mr. V put an arm around Billy's shoulder and led him away. "Billy, if you ever hope to take over this business, you need to come to terms with certain unsavory realities."

Billy knocked his father's arm off. "But I don't want to take over! I never did. That's how this all got started in the first place."

"We'll talk about it later, son."

It was now or never—time for Plan B. Bird whistled loudly to signal Mochabean. She tensed every muscle, ready to jump into action the second her backup man burst in and caused a distraction. There was no telling exactly what would happen. But whatever happened, she would need to move fast.

Nothing happened.

A few seconds later, there was a muted thump from the other side of a nearby emergency exit. Everyone turned to the door. It thump, thump, thumped three more times, then went silent.

On the other side of the emergency exit Mochabean rattled the doorknob violently. "It won't open! It's locked!" his muffled voice announced from outside.

"Christ on a crutch, he's just a big, dumb sack of beef jerky," Bird sighed. So much for a last-minute rescue. It wasn't exactly that she was disappointed, since she'd learned long ago that she couldn't count on anyone but herself. But it would have been nice, just once, to have someone come through for her.

But he hadn't, and now she was going to die.

"After you finish with her, go take care of the cavalry out there," William Veach ordered his remaining bodyguard.

"No problem, boss." He aimed his gun at Bird's heart. "Nothing personal. I'll make it quick."

It's funny, for as stressed out as she was most of the time, Bird felt oddly calm at this, the final moment of her life. Maybe it was because Ruby was safely away from here. Jesse was still outside, but he'd be OK; he was far enough away that they wouldn't notice him. And Mochabean, well, fuck Mochabean. Best of all, she'd never have to deal with coming out to her mom. Sweet Jesus, that was a relief.

The bodyguard hesitated when he saw the bounty hunter smiling. For some reason her eyes were closed, and she had the most serene, peaceful look on her face. Not at all what one would expect from someone who was about to be shot. Just the same, he had to shoot her, or he'd end up like his pal Goldie.

Then a clown wandered into their midst. "Anyone know where they keep the confetti around here?" the clown asked innocently.

They were all surprised, to say the least. It was William Veach who took the lead and asked the obvious question: "And who the hell are you?"

"Buenos dias," said a too cheery voice. "I'm Chili. I need

confetti for my piñatas. Oh, I see it. Don't mind me." The clown skipped over to a sack of the vibrant stuff. She winked at a dumbfounded Bird as she went past.

"Ruby . . . ?" Bird whispered.

The bodyguard lowered his gun, unsure of the proper protocol to follow for when a clown interrupted a hit. It was a first for him. He looked to Mr. V for direction and shrugged.

"Look . . . Chili, was it?" Veach said. "I suggest you leave immediately. The Party Palace is closed temporarily. Come back tomorrow."

"Don't mind me. I'll be done in a jiff." Ruby flip-flopped her way to another sack, nothing but a goofy clown, harmlessness, no threat here, no sir.

William Veach grabbed her arm as she skipped past him. "I said leave."

Ruby looked down at the hand gripping her, then up at the grabby guy himself. The guy who had her kidnapped. The guy who was about to have her big sister shot. The guy who, at the moment, she hated more than any other person in the whole entire world. The smile disappeared from her made-up face. "Snake slithers free and strikes," Ruby said.

"Snake what?" Veach sneered at her.

Ruby shifted her body and easily snatched her arm away from his grip. Still turning, she kicked out to the bodyguard who stood nearby and knocked the gun out of his hand. The gun rattled away, oddly enough into the same pile of realistic-looking water pistols where Big Bertha was now hiding. In the blink of an eye, Ruby had freed herself from one man and disarmed another.

William Veach, Billy, the bodyguard—even Bird, who was beginning to have some idea of what her little sister could do—all stared in shock at the clown with the Bruce Lee moves.

"Ruby Blacker, professional badass," she said smugly, hands at her hips.

Imagine being a "pro" and getting disarmed by a clown. It would stick in anybody's craw. The bodyguard, no doubt humiliated at how quickly he had lost his gun, took a swing at Ruby. She had made him look bad in front of his boss, and done so in mascara and an orange wig.

Ruby dodged his fist easily and kicked him in the groin. Yet, surprisingly, he didn't go down immediately. Instead, his face burning red with anger and pain, he lunged at Ruby. But he was too slow. She sidestepped, delivered a palm to his nose, breaking it, and kicked him in the nuts a second time. And he still didn't go down. Was this guy wearing a cup? Was he a eunuch?

He was slow, that was for certain. Ruby hammered his head before he could react, and this time he swayed uncertainly on his legs. He was tough, but she was fast, accurate, and persistent. In the end, it was no contest.

"I'll break your clown face . . . you goddamned freak . . . " The bodyguard was all but gone now. He could barely stay on his feet.

William Veach had come to realize he couldn't depend on his bodyguards for much of anything. He was on hands and knees on the floor, searching through the pile of plastic guns for something that would shoot more than water. At least two of the weapons in there were real. It was tough going, though. The manufacturer had made the toys so realistic that you couldn't tell if they were real or not just by looking at them. To make matters worse, each pistol was weighted down, to give the heft of a real gun. What kind of society was this when toy makers strived to make their products look and feel as much like a real gun as possible? It was enough to make a concerned parent (and head of an L.A. criminal organization) scream in frustration. "I'm going to find whoever made these and cut his balls off!" He pulled the trigger on a gun, but got only a stream of liquid as a result. Veach threw the toy aside angrily.

Bird tackled the crime lord, both of them rolling on the floor and sending toy pistols scattering everywhere.

Meanwhile, Ruby went in for the kill with her diminishing adversary. She jabbed at his face, but he actually managed to block this one. His victory was short-lived, however, since the move was just a bluff to distract him. Ruby followed through with her finishing move: a third and final kick to the jewels.

The bodyguard had reached his limit; clearly, three was the magic number when it came to violent punts to the groin. He uttered a final "Fuckin' clown . . . " and collapsed on the floor in a curled-up ball.

Billy looked on helplessly at the commotion around him. It was unclear exactly whose side he was on: the criminals out to kill innocent people or the bounty hunters trying to land him in jail.

In the midst of all the turmoil, the emergency exit doorknob began rattling violently again.

•

Just outside, Mochabean had his ear to the door. Muffled voices could be heard from inside the warehouse, but it was unclear what they were saying. "So should I wait for another signal here or what?" he yelled as loudly as possible.

When there was no response, he put his ear to the door again. This time there was definitely the sound of a fist connecting with bone, probably lower jaw. "Dammit, Bird, you better save some for me!"

Bam, bam, bam—he kicked at the metal door with his giant foot, but it wouldn't budge. He pounded on it with his fist. He slammed his shoulder against it, using his considerable body mass as a battering ram.

And in the end, there was not so much as a dent. "Huh, pretty good door, right there," he said with genuine admiration.

•

William Veach violently kicked Bird away. She slammed against a wall, then bounced off a wooden crate, finally landing on the cement floor with a dull crack. Some men had reservations about hitting a woman; he had no such scruples. Besides, she certainly wasn't holding back with him. The bounty hunter had already given him a black eye, scratched his face bloody, and nearly ripped his throat out. Honestly, who fought like that?

"Dad, should I . . . ," Billy started.

"Stay out of it, boy. I'll handle this." William Veach smiled, blood running down his face. He grabbed a crowbar off a crate and walked toward the groaning body of Bird Blacker. "Just like the old days. Now this is my kind of workout." He raised the metal bar in the air, ready to bash in the troublesome woman's head, when suddenly, a whistle pierced the air and stopped him. He turned and saw the clown aiming a gun at him.

"Hold it!" Ruby called out. "No, wait—freeze? Yeah, that's what you say. Freeze!"

William Veach shook his head at the girl. "Nice toy. Very realistic, aren't they?" He turned back to Bird, who was quickly regaining her wits.

Blam!

Veach flinched and spun around to find the clown aiming the gun in the air. A real gun, with smoke curling from the barrel.

She'd found one of the two handguns in the mound of toys.

"Put that down before you hurt yourself, kid." Veach lowered the crowbar to his side. He slowly walked toward Ruby and tried his calming voice once again. "Just set it down and we'll talk, OK? That's a complicated thing you're holding in your hands."

Ruby chambered a round and aimed it at his chest. "I think I've got it figured out. Now get down on the floor."

"Kid, you don't know what you're doing."

Blam!—the shot dug into a box inches to William Veach's left. Red balloon guts spilled out of the mortally wounded container.

"All right, fine," he quickly said. "I'm getting down. See? Not moving." He set the crowbar down and lay on the cold floor.

Bird pulled out a pair of handcuffs and snapped them on William Veach's wrists behind his back. "I assume this is not a new experience for you," she said as she squeezed the cuffs extra tight. She yanked him to his feet and found Ruby smiling from ear to ear.

Bird stared at her sister. Her sister who for some reason was dressed as a clown. The sister whom Bird had come to rescue, but who instead ended up rescuing her. And now there she was smiling with relief that it was all over.

"God, that was . . . ," Ruby said.

Poor kid's probably scared half to death, Bird thought.

" . . . so much fun!" the clown exclaimed joyfully.

Bird then realized she had absolutely no idea how Ruby's mind worked, and probably never would. "What are you wearing?" she asked her younger sister.

"My disguise—a clown in a party-supply store. I figured they'd never notice me sneak back in this way. Pretty clever, huh?"

Bird had to admit it was indeed clever. She herself would not have considered such a ruse to get back into the warehouse. In fact, she would not have come back at all. "If you escaped, why didn't you just go to the police?"

After a pause, Ruby said, "I don't know. I guess it never occurred to me. Besides, this way seems more fun, don't you think?"

Bird sighed. "Are you sure you're not adopted?"

There was a sudden crack of a gunshot, and Ruby's gun was knocked clean from her hand.

"Yeaich!" She waved her hand around from the stinging pain.

Kaya stood in a dark corner of the room, smoking gun in hand.

"Told you I could make the shot."

William Veach pulled away from Bird. "The keys," he demanded. Bird reluctantly opened the cuffs and set him free.

"I guess you are good for something after all," Veach said to his daughter. But instead of going toward her to thank her, he walked over to his son, Billy, who was crouching behind some boxes, hoping to go unnoticed in the commotion. He was still a fugitive. "Are you all right, boy?" Veach patted him down, looking for bruises or scratches.

"I'm OK. I mean, I guess . . . "

"Good," Veach said. He turned to Kaya, then to the Blacker sisters. "Kill them both. I've had enough of this."

Kaya grinned, using the cold smile she had inherited from her father. She held up her gun, but she did not fire.

"What are you waiting for? Shoot!" William Veach yelled at her.

Bird shoved her sister behind her, using her own body as a shield. They had been so close to getting out of there. She couldn't believe it was all for nothing. Think fast, do something, anything.

"Kaya, please, I thought we had something special," Bird said, holding up her hand. Ruby, meanwhile, scrunched her brow: they had something special?

Another gunshot echoed in the warehouse.

Bird and Ruby both flinched and shut their eyes at the sound of the blast . . .

When Bird opened hers, she was surprised to find no extra holes in her body. Ruby was intact as well.

Meanwhile, Billy looked down at himself and, inexplicably, saw a red stain growing on his chest. The look on his face said, Why is there a red stain on my shirt? Where had it come from?

"What are you—" William Veach turned to his son, saw the wound. "Dear God."

Billy reached down, touched the stain, and saw that it was blood. With a confused expression, he held up a bloody hand to his father. "Dad?" Then the younger Veach toppled over.

"N-o-o-o!" the crime lord screamed out in agony. He quickly grabbed his son, and cradled his head in his lap.

Still in a secluded corner, Kaya grinned as dark shadows danced upon her maniacal face. Something inside of her had cracked, had broken beyond repair after years of abuse and neglect. Of love unrequited no matter how many people she maimed or killed for this man who rewarded her only with scorn and disdain, and who would never call her "daughter." "Now I'm all the family you have left, sir." Kaya's voice rang hollow, barren of what little humanity she previously may have possessed.

"You crazy bitch! You're no blood of mine." William Veach held his son, whose own blood now soiled his shirt.

"I always knew it would come to this," Kaya said. "But I was hoping you'd wise up, stop wasting your attention on him. That you'd see I'm the one who really loves you."

"Kaya, I swear by all that's holy," Veach spat the words at her with all the rage and hatred he could muster, "if he dies, I'll kill you with my bare hands."

Kaya cocked her head to the side, grinning as if she'd just remembered the punch line to a joke heard long ago. "You know what's funny, Dad?" She raised her gun once more. "I believe you would."

Blam!

The shot hit William Veach square in the chest. He fell over on top of Billy, the blood of father and son now mixing on the floor as they died in each other's arms.

"Oh. My. God," Ruby whispered, as she squeezed down on her sister's arm with a death grip. "Bird?"

"Let me think," Bird replied. But she was at a loss. Never, in all her years as a police officer or bounty hunter, had she been witness to anything even remotely like this scene. She did, however, have one trusty axiom she could fall back on: "When in doubt, get the hell out." Kaya had gone certifiably batshit. All they could hope to do was escape and figure out their next step later. Bird pulled her sister and slowly backed away toward the hallway that led out of the warehouse. They didn't get far.

Kaya aimed her gun at Bird and Ruby without even looking at them, her gaze still on her dying father and half brother. "You should have listened to me, Bird," Kaya said. "I warned you to stay out of this. Now I have no choice. Talk about a psycho ex-girlfriend, huh?"

Before Bird could respond, Ruby exclaimed, "Wait! I want— I want another shot. Me and you, hand to hand."

"Girl, shut the hell up," Bird hissed at her foolish sister. Then she turned to Kaya. "Don't listen to her. She's young, she's ignorant—she's from Texas."

•

From the relative comfort of his van's driver's chair, Jesse could see a very large object running around the Party Palace warehouse. Mochabean hoofed it to the side of the building. He looked for a door or other opening, but there was none to be found, other than the main entrance and the emergency rear exit he had failed to bash open. Next, the bald man tried jumping up at open windows. Alas, a body such as his was further proof that white (enormously large) men can't jump, leaving every window far out of reach.

"I bet that gorilla missed the signal," Jesse said derisively.

Finally, Mochabean ran back to the van. He slid the door open and rummaged in the back. "You got a tire iron in here?"

Jesse reached under his seat and pulled out a metal bar. "You mean like this?"

Mochabean grabbed the tire iron, slapped it against his palm. "This'll do."

"What do you need it for?"

"Back door's locked. I gotta break in."

Iron in hand, the giant ran back to the rear of the warehouse.

"Why don't you . . . ," Jesse called out, but Mochabean was out of earshot, "just go in the front door? Big dope."

17

HAND TO HAND

"YOU WANT TO FIGHT me, little girl?" Kaya asked Ruby. The killer smiled like she'd just been offered a free steak dinner and her choice of dessert.

"This little girl can take you down, and you know it." Ruby pushed past Bird.

The bounty hunter grabbed Ruby's hand and tried backing away slowly again. "She's kidding. We don't care what happened here—none of our business."

"Uh-uh, you're not going anywhere." Kaya pointed the gun at them. "All right, sweetheart, I'm kind of curious to see what you've got." She strode over to the Blacker sisters and paused right in front of Bird.

For a split second Bird thought she recognized something in that look, something that could have been. Then the look was gone, replaced by an emptiness as cold as the vacuum of space.

"But first . . ." Kaya slapped Bird's own cuffs on her wrist and secured her to a water pipe on the warehouse wall, then pocketed the keys. "Can't have you interfering. That wouldn't be fair." Then the killer holstered her gun and waited in the center of the warehouse, still as a lifeless statue.

"When are you going to learn to keep your mouth shut?" Bird hissed at her impetuous sister.

"Trust me." Ruby winked. "I can do this."

The two women faced each other in the middle of the warehouse. Kaya versus Ruby—the professional killer versus the young, fast fighter.

"I should warn you," Ruby said. "I usually spar with guys twice my size. And I always win."

From perfect stillness, Kaya whipped a kick to Ruby's head!

Ruby barely ducked in time and stumbled away. She quickly regained her balance and started dancing around on her feet, like a boxer.

"I killed five men in the past year alone," Kaya said with her subzero smile. She peered at the bodies of William and Billy Veach. "Make that seven."

"Dammit, Ruby," a frustrated Bird called out. "Pay attention out there. This isn't one of your martial arts meets. There are no rules!" Bird yanked forcefully at the handcuffs linking her to the wall. They held her tight.

Ruby bounced around the stationary Kaya, testing her defenses, looking for an opening. The girl attacked with a punch-kick combo.

Kaya blocked easily and countered with a flurry of vicious punches.

The smaller Ruby evaded them, but was pushed back. Then she backflipped away, out of Kaya's reach.

"You going for the gold, slugger? We fighting here, or trying out for the Olympics?"

"Wah-taaah!" cried Ruby in her best martial arts yell, as she leaped into a magnificent flying kick. It was perfect form, combining grace, speed, and power—Bruce Lee would have been proud.

Kaya merely sidestepped at the last second and let the girl

fly by harmlessly. Then she swept Ruby's feet out from under her the instant she touched down.

Ruby rolled away to safety, scarcely evading several stomps from Kaya's foot. The girl then sprang back on her feet. She wiped a bead of sweat from her forehead and considered her opponent.

Kaya stood relaxed and ready, one arm at her hip. She wasn't breathing hard; she hadn't broken a sweat. Even her designer suit still looked impeccable, not a wrinkle on it. No sign of effort, certainly no sign that she was on the losing end of a hand-to-hand slugfest. Only that aloof, frosty smile of hers.

"OK, you're good," Ruby conceded. "Maybe better than I thought."

"Oh, my dear," she turned her body sideways and bent her left leg slightly, like a spring building power, "I'm much more than good." Kaya blasted Ruby with three high kicks to the head.

The girl was ready, blocking the kicks with her arms, but wasn't expecting a fourth kick that pummeled her in the stomach with such force that it propelled Ruby clean off her feet. There was no acrobatic moves to recover from such a blow; all she could do was ride the force as it sent her flying. Ruby crashed into a stack of cardboard boxes.

"You still had so much to learn. Pity to waste such potential." Kaya strolled leisurely toward her prey. Luckily, the killer preferred sensible shoes over heels, or her kick would have hurt a hell of a lot worse.

Bird pulled madly at the cuffs keeping her from assisting her sister. It was torture, not being able to get in there and help—even if only to take a couple of the knocks in place of Ruby. Her pale skin was flushed; her dark hair, usually pulled back tight, hung in strands across her face. Her clothes had gone from crisply pressed to bag-lady chic. She was a mess and she didn't care. The only thought that burned bright as a star in her mind was, Help Ruby! "Get out of here!" she screamed at her little sister. "For once in your life, please listen to me. Do whatever you have to, but get out!" Like a chained and half-crazed animal, Bird yanked at the cuffs so hard that her wrists were bleeding. "Kaya, leave her alone!" she said desperately.

If she heard, Kaya did not show it. She kicked the prone Ruby and sent her rolling toward her sister. Ruby crawled the rest of the way to where Bird was handcuffed. The girl pulled herself until she was within arm's reach, then whispered to Bird, "Do you still have that hand soap?"

"What?" Bird wasn't sure she had understood the question. "Listen, just get up and go. I'll try to distract her."

"Bird, trust me!" Ruby insisted. She looked over her shoulder; Kaya was slowly making her way toward them. "Gimme a big glop of the stuff, right in my palms." She held out her hands.

"Hey, Ruby, I'm kinda handcuffed."

"Oh, right." Ruby fished in her sister's pocket, then quickly pumped a large helping of the powerful hand disinfectant onto each of her palms.

Ruby closed her fists enough to hide the stuff, but not so much that it spilled out between her fingers. "Good. Now, try to distract her. All I need is half a second."

"What are you up to?" Bird asked.

"If you can't beat a stronger opponent, you outsmart them." Ruby stood as best she could and faced Kaya, who was almost upon her again. "Remember," she whispered, "buy me some time."

Kaya was once again within striking distance with those deadly limbs of hers. One more hit from her, and Ruby would be down for the count, or worse. Kaya stared at Ruby with dead eyes and clenched her hands into iron fists, her knuckles cracking loudly.

Sweet Lord above, Bird pondered how she ever lived to the ripe old age of thirty (cough), twenty-eight. It seemed her life was a never-ending series of attempts on her life or on that of someone close to her. How had an already bad situation turned this shade of shit? Two days ago the biggest problem Bird had was getting Vicky to pay her full fee. Now she'd gone from having a kidnapped sister to a life-and-death hand-to-hand fight. If she were the sort of person who put stock in karma, Bird must have been someone truly unsavory in a past life to be so deep in it now. Perhaps she was a pirate, a Nazi, or one of the very first telemarketers.

Kaya grabbed Ruby's hair with one hand and drew back the other to deliver a final, fatal strike to the girl, who could barely stand on her rubbery legs. Bird, desperate to stop the woman, called out the first thing that popped into her mind: "Kaya, I love you! I always have!"

Kaya paused. She looked at Bird with a spark of hope in her eyes, a hope that someone somewhere actually gave two damns about a wretch like her. Her father didn't, her brother didn't—and they both had paid the price. Her mother might have, but Kaya didn't really remember much about her mother; she had died when Kaya was a girl. But now Bird had said the words no one had ever uttered to Kaya in any relationship she'd ever had. Those three little words were enough to distract the killer for a split second.

A split second was all the time Ruby needed. She pulled away, leaving only an orange clown wig in Kaya's grasp, then slapped Kaya across the eyes with a handful of the industrial cleaner her sister had squirted in her palms. For the soap to be strong enough to keep a germophobe like Bird happy, it had to be just short of sulfuric acid. No More Tears, it certainly wasn't.

"Ahh, you little bitch!" Kaya clutched at her burning eyes. She rubbed and wiped them and could scarcely open them. When she did open one, it was bloodshot, red and angry. She couldn't see two feet in front of her, let alone keep fighting. "Fuck, it burns! What is this—what did you to me?"

"I outsmarted my opponent," the girl said. "Just like you said." Ruby didn't hesitate. Knowing that sooner or later Kaya would regain enough vision to once again threaten her and her sister, she acted quickly, efficiently, with no remorse. She grabbed Kaya's flailing arm, flipped her, and slammed her down hard against the concrete floor.

Even so, Kaya would not stay down. She lurched to her feet and swung her fists blindly, looking for a lucky shot. "You're dead, girl. That's not a threat, it's a promise! There's nowhere you can hide that I won't find you."

"That's about enough lip from you, lady." Ruby jabbed Kaya in the throat with stiffened fingers, sending the woman gasping for breath. Her opponent was now blind and incapacitated, effectively out of commission. But Ruby wasn't taking any chances. One last roundhouse kick express-delivered to Kaya's head sent her crashing into a stack of tubes. And it was lights-out for Kaya—the professional assassin soundly defeated by a teenage girl.

Ruby picked up her clown wig off the floor and dusted it off. "Better not have damaged this. I'll lose my deposit."

"Sweet baby Jesus," whispered an astonished Bird. "I can't believe you did it."

Ruby took the handcuff keys from Kaya's pocket and walked over to her sister.

"Told you I could take her." She unlocked Bird from her

bonds. Ruby stopped to consider something. "What was that she said about being your ex-girlfriend?"

"I—I don't know." No, no, no, no. The bad guys were all down for the count, and all Bird had to do was walk out of there and she'd be home free. She couldn't let her younger sister out her to her family now, not now when everything could go back to the way it was before. "The woman is obviously crazy. She shot her own father, for Pete's sake."

"Well, yeah, but . . . why did you tell her you love her? I mean, where did that come from? It's kind of weird."

"Look, you wanted a distraction, and that's what I gave you. It's the only thing I could think of." Bird tried to sound as casual as possible to throw Ruby off the trail, but there was an edge to her voice, an anxiety she couldn't hide. So she used the same tactic: distraction. "Help me look for Vicky's gun. She'll make me pay for it if I don't bring it back."

"It just seems odd, her saying what she did and then you saying . . . " Ruby trailed off. She was no fool—young and brash, yes, but no fool. Sooner or later she'd catch on.

"We'll talk about it later." Inquisitiveness was a Blacker family trait, and Bird knew her sister was not likely to drop the matter outright. She was desperate to distract her. "Forget the gun. Let's just get out while we still can. There's no telling who else might show up." Bird pushed her sister toward the hallway exit. But they didn't get far.

"Oh, but it's not over yet, ladies," a familiar voice croaked. Bruised and bloody, with eyes red as the devil's own, Kaya propped herself up into a sitting position. Maybe she was too drained to walk up and finish the Blacker girls, but she could still hold a gun in her hand.

"Whoa, she is hard-core," Ruby said with admiration, despite herself.

"Forget her, she probably can't see straight." Bird made for the exit. A gunshot to the floor in front of her stopped her instantly.

"I can see well enough," Kaya said.

"Whack job, am I gonna have to put you down a second time?" Ruby rolled up the sleeves on her clown shirt, ready to mix it up again.

Blam!—the bullet missed her head by an atom, blowing back the surprised girl's hair.

"Crap in a hat!" Too far to run for the hallway, Bird grabbed Ruby and pulled her behind a nearby large crate. They were safe, for the moment.

Blam! Blam!—two more shots dug into the wooden container. Thankfully, whatever party item the crate carried was enough to stop Kaya's shots, but she had them pinned down good. There was nowhere they could go without finding a bullet waiting for them. The women were trapped behind the crate, and Ruby wasn't keen on staying there.

"What happened to keeping things fair?" Ruby called out to her former sparring partner. She looked out over the edge of the crate and was pulled back down an instant before another bullet splintered the very same spot her head had been occupying.

Bird held the girl's head with both hands and looked her in the eyes. "Can't you shut your trap for five minutes?"

"Let go, you're hurting me." Ruby shoved her sister away. "And I just saved your life too."

"Yeah? Well now you're going to get us both killed." Bird shoved her sister right back. "Great job."

"At least I don't hide from my problems." Shove.

"You don't know the first thing about real problems." Push.

"I was kidnapped at gunpoint—I think that qualifies." Shove.

"And we'd already be out of here if you'd listened to me." Push.

Blam! This time the shot went right through the crate and came out the other end, directly between the Blacker sisters.

"Enough," Kaya yelled. "You two are giving me a headache."

Bird and Ruby pressed against the crate, though it no longer seemed all that safe a place to be hiding.

•

Meanwhile, Mochabean was still determined to get into the warehouse and join in on the action. By now, there had been crashes and gunshots and all sorts of fun noises coming from inside. He bashed at the metal door with the crowbar he'd found in the van. "Hoo-yeah, make way for Mochabean."

The door dented and sparked with each blow. Finally, it began to buckle around the doorknob, where he was concentrating his strikes. A few more hits and he'd be in. "There better be some ass left in there for me to kick. I mean it, Bird. I didn't come all the way out here for nothing."

•

Bird and Ruby weren't having nearly as much fun as Mochabean might have thought. They huddled behind the crate, far, far from the nearest exit. But at least the shooting had stopped. Maybe Kaya had run out of ammo? Bird really wished now she had kept track of the shots fired. Somehow, however, it never occurred to her to count bullets when she was busy dodging them. Nevertheless, maybe luck was on her side.

"I'm going to run out and get her attention," Bird told her

sister. "When I do, you head straight for the door. Don't look back and don't stop for anything. Understand?"

"Are you sure about this?" Ruby looked worried.

"I think she's out of bullets."

"You think, or you know?"

"I'm 90 percent sure." Bird smiled weakly. "Ready? Here we go." She leaned her head out the side of the crate and was greeted by a cloud of wood chips as a shot splintered the side of the container. Bird quickly ducked back.

"I see you, little Ladybird," the assassin called out from her sitting position.

"Your math sucks," Ruby informed her sister.

"Maybe that wasn't such a hot idea," Bird conceded.

"Got a plan B?" Ruby asked.

"Plan B? I've pretty much run out of alphabet here."

"So what are you going to do?" Her sister looked at her with the same expression as when they were kids, like when Ruby broke a neighbor's window with a baseball and she expected her big sister to somehow bail her out.

"What am I going to do?" Bird looked at her baby sister and knew "I don't know" wouldn't cut it. "I'll do what I do best: I'll wing it."

She scanned the area for anything that could possibly provide them with some help. Balloons: no help there. Piñatas: cute but useless. Birthday candles: maybe if she had a jug of gasoline. Water guns: both futile and infuriating because they looked so damned real that . . . One of the guns spilled on the floor nearby grabbed her attention. It was bigger than the rest, much bigger. Big Bertha. She couldn't help but smile. With that monstrosity in hand, they had a real chance of escape. She could even blast a hole in the wall and make her own exit, if need be. But she was so far away, about twenty feet. She'd never reach Bertha without getting ventilated by Kaya.

Then there was William Veach. Bird could see he was still breathing, his chest rising and falling slightly as he lay in a pool of blood by his son's body. Kaya had left her father for dead, but he may yet be their salvation. "Hey, Veach," Bird whispered. "You still alive? Veach!"

The man stirred but was in no condition to chat. Severe blood loss will do that to you.

"I thought you should know, the psycho who shot you and your son is gonna walk out of here clean and clear."

Spurred on by a pure and burning rage, William Veach looked up and locked eyes with Bird.

"Look, I softened her up for you." She nodded at Kaya, who looked like she'd been playing tag with a freight train. Nevertheless, she was in much better shape than William Veach, and far better off than his son, Billy.

Kaya was so intent on the Blacker sisters, she didn't notice her father was stirring.

"But she's still gonna walk right out of here," Bird whispered. "Unless, of course, you stop her."

"Bird, what are you doing?" Ruby pulled at her sleeve. "He's the bad guy."

Bird shushed her.

"Plus he's half dead. What's he going to do, bleed on her?"

"Will you just zip your beak for once in your life, and let me do what I have to do?"

Ruby backed off.

Bird continued to urge Veach. "You gonna let her walk out of here after what she did? After she killed your boy?"

Veach slowly, achingly, reached down his leg, to a hidden gun tucked away in an ankle holster. While still on his back, he aimed a shaking hand at Kaya.

"Get ready to run," Bird warned her sister.

Blam!—the shot pocked the cement floor a few inches from Kaya's feet and stole her attention away from the hiding Blacker girls.

"My only son!" Veach cried out, incensed.

"Now you show interest in me?" Kaya shot back.

"Come on, they're both off their nut." Bird took hold of Ruby's hand, and they both made for the hallway, which would lead them to the front office and out of the building.

"Die, animal!" Veach fired again and again until one slug found its way to Kaya's leg. She barely flinched and kept firing back at her father.

Ruby and Bird, meantime, were out of the main warehouse and running down the long hallway toward the exit. Ruby stopped midway. "Bird, what about—"

"Shut up and run, you pain in the ass!" she said as she kept dashing and pulled Ruby alongside her.

Back in the warehouse, the metal door of the emergency exit flew open with a loud clang. Then a bald behemoth burst through the entry with a crowbar, bent from abuse, gripped in his hand and a scowl, perfected from much use, on his face. "Mochabean's here, let the ass-kicking begin!"

"That's the last time you hurt me, Father." Kaya emphasized the word, which he never let her use, to remind him both that she was family, no matter how much he hated to admit it, and, more important, that he no longer had any say in what she could or could not do. Which was unfortunate for him, because at the moment what she wanted to do was kill him.

This, of course, was all lost on Mochabean, who as usual was two steps behind everyone else. "Father? What?"

Kaya's final shot hit William Veach, and the rest of his life spilled out of him. But not before he got off his last shot, which strayed from its intended target. Instead, the bullet hit a propane tank behind Kaya.

Instantly, the entire combustible stack exploded around her. The fireball devoured Kaya, leaped across the room, and engulfed William Veach. In that sudden flash of heat and smoke, father and daughter were finally united, closer in death than they had ever been in life.

Then the fireball kept going.

"Oh, shi—" The explosion blasted Mochabean back out the emergency exit door, after all the time and effort he had spent to get in.

The inferno roared down the hallway Bird and Ruby had taken. The blast reached them as they were steps before making it to the exit. Both women flew out the door and into the parking lot outside, blown upward by the explosion. As they flailed through the air, the world decelerated into slow motion: Bird's face was frozen in a mask of terror as she was lifted clean off the ground. Ruby, meanwhile, looked almost joyful as the blast wave carried her aloft.

18

EXPLOSIONS ARE EASY, LANDING IS HARD

JESSE SAW THE WHOLE thing from a safe distance—the explosion, the Amazing Flying Blacker Sisters, everything. The thundering blast was even strong enough to shake the van, the old shocks squealing as it rocked back and forth. "What in the name of Krishna . . . " He jumped out and ran to the warehouse parking lot to try to help.

The flight was a bumpy one, but it was the landing that really hurt. Bird and Ruby hit the pavement, rolled several times, and ended up on their backs next to each other facing opposite directions. All around them it rained down candy, confetti, and bits of multicolored streamers from the sky.

"You OK?" Bird had her eyes closed. It hurt too much to try to open them. And besides, she'd much rather forget most of what she'd seen the past few days anyway.

"Think so . . . You?" Ruby, on the other hand, had her eyes wide open so as not to miss a single detail of her adventure. She was breathing hard, but out of fear or excitement—or both— who knew?

"I still got my legs?"

Ruby turned her head and saw Bird's shoes, scuffed and scratched. Her legs were there as well, though the pants had lost their crease. "Yeah, I see them."

"Good. That must be where the shooting pain is coming from."

Jesse reached Bird and Ruby and fluttered from one to the other, unsure which one to assist first, or for that matter what to do to help them. "Are you guys alive?" He took Bird's hand and held it to his ear. Then he did the same against his other ear.

Bird finally opened her eyes after almost dying in a fiery explosion, and the first thing she saw was Jesse's goofy face looking down at her with concern. For some reason, he seemed to be rubbing her hand against the sides of his face. Oh, God, he wasn't about to declare his love for her, was he? First her ex tries to kill her, and now a straight guy falls for her. That would just be the cherry on top. "What are you doing?" she asked.

"I'm checking for a pulse, man."

She pulled her hand away. "Don't worry about it. I have one."

"OK, man, it's cool. Just trying to help. Ruby, how you doing, little lady?" He took Ruby's hand and "checked her pulse" as well.

"Did you see how far we flew?" she said cheerfully from her prone position.

"I saw it all the way from the van. That was some major air time! Fwoosh—right across the parking lot like a couple of mighty condors!" He made an arching motion with his hand. "Just about the coolest damned thing I've ever seen."

"I know, it was awesome!" She smiled blissfully, the way a child does the first time she sees Disneyland. Compared to her sedate life back in Texas, her time in Los Angeles with her big sister was indeed a trip to a magical kingdom.

Jesse smiled down at Ruby's enthusiastic face as he held her hand to his ear. Bird couldn't help but notice that they were smiling at each other for an uncomfortably long moment (uncomfortable for Bird, anyway). It also didn't escape her notice that her sister wasn't pulling her hand away from Jesse's grip, that she didn't seem to mind at all. Her baby sister and Jesse . . . ?

"Don't worry about me, it's just my spinal cord that hurts!" Bird said and pulled on Jesse's leg. "I'm sure I can get another one somewhere."

It was enough to drag Jesse's attention away from Ruby, Bird's inexperienced and way-too-naive little sister, and back onto her. Jesse released Ruby's hand and came to check on Bird. "But you're not gonna die, right?"

"Well, it's tough to say with spinal cords . . . ," she answered.

"Cool." Jesse eyed the candy that littered the lot and the streamers and confetti that still fell all around them. "Because I gotta go." He ran off to collect all the goodies that rained down like gifts from heaven.

"Bird?" Ruby called.

"Yeah."

"How did you know that guy had a gun hidden away?"

"Because he was a douche bag." She sighed. "I know well, unfortunately. I track them down for a living." Hard to believe Bird had wanted to be a ballet dancer when she was a child. That or a race-car driver. Certainly, she had never wanted to grow up and track down douche bags for a living as she did now. That particular thought elicited another, even longer sigh.

For a long moment, Ruby was uncharacteristically silent. Bird hoped her sister had forgotten about some of the things said in the warehouse, or at least that she would be too distracted to think about them. But no, if anything Ruby was puzzling it all together.

Finally, Ruby said matter-of-factly, "That woman back there, she said she was your ex." She looked at Bird expectantly.

"Crazy people tend to say crazy things." Bird held her breath, wishing that would be the end of the matter.

"Are you . . . ," Ruby chose her next words carefully, "a gay or lesbian?"

"Now's not the time." She sighed.

"I just . . . Is that why you never call home, why you never visit us?" The young girl tried to keep an even tone, but the hurt was there for anyone to hear.

Bird bit her lip and said nothing. Fuck, she thought. Fuck, fuck, triple-time fuck!

"Does Mom know?" Ruby asked.

"Are you kidding me? She'd have a stroke."

And there it was: she'd all but announced to her sister that she, Ladybird Blacker, was a dyke. A gay or lesbian. For better of worse—and who are we kidding, it was no doubt for worse—there was no taking it back now. For all intents and purposes, Bird was out. She shut her eyes tight and waited for the inevitable shit storm to begin.

"Well, I'm cool with it."

There had to be something wrong with her hearing, because it sounded like Ruby said, "I'm cool with it." When she knew Ruby's words had to have been more along the lines of, "I'm telling Mom. You are so fucked."

"What did you say?"

"Look, half the girls I know in college are bi—it's like they want to test-drive different models before they decide on a final purchase. But, can I suggest something to make your life easier?"

"What's that?" Her eyes slit suspiciously.

"Next time, how about trying to date someone—"

"What, with a penis?" Bird said cynically. "I am not bisexual. I have no interest in test-driving a different model, I don't want to kick the tires, or look under the hood at . . . the dipstick."

"I was going to say, someone who's not a homicidal maniac. So if you break up they won't try to kill you."

"Oh. Yes, that sounds reasonable." All things considered, Ruby had taken the news that her big sister is a lesbian quite well. In fact, maybe Bird had misjudged all her family's open-mindedness. "You really don't care that I'm gay?"

"When people are trying to kill you, it tends to put things in perspective. Whatever makes you happy is fine with me. Who you choose to, uh, you know . . . "

"Yes, thank you, I get it." Bird put a quick end to that awkward direction in conversation. "Do me a favor: Don't tell Mom? She's kind of . . . old-fashioned."

"Yeah, I think to her, love means driving the people you care about crazy. We have to be the most screwed-up family in America."

Bird smiled to herself. "I don't know about that. At least I've never shot my sibling out of murderous jealousy. So far."

Between the sisters and the warehouse, Jesse ran around the parking lot like a child, leaping and grabbing at the streamers and confetti raining down and stuffing candy in his pockets. "It's beautiful, man." He giggled and skipped about. "It's like the dreams I used to have as a kid!"

"My partner, ladies and gentlemen," Bird said sarcastically. "The guy I trust with my life on a daily basis."

"He's something, all right." Ruby shook her head and smiled. Then she saw someone behind Jesse, someone big lumbering toward them. "Uh, Bird?"

It was Mochabean, his clothes charred, confetti stuck to his bald head, with a slight limp in his right leg. And he did not look pleased.

"Trouble coming this way." Ruby raised herself on her elbows. "Come on, partner, we can take him together." She got a few more inches off the ground, then fell back dizzy. "Maybe not. Give me a second. I'll be ready soon as the world stops spinning."

Bird craned her neck and saw Mochabean. "Don't worry about him. I'm fairly sure he's with us."

"He is?"

"I said 'fairly,' didn't I?"

As Mochabean got closer Bird could see he was sucking on a lollipop. Lollipops were a positive sign, weren't they? Then again, he was still scowling, and she had no trouble picturing Mochabean pummeling someone to death even as he sucked on a lollipop. It really could go either way at this point, so she took a deep breath and hoped for the best, which she considered a sign of personal growth, since normally she would have winced and expected the worst.

Mochabean blocked the sun as he stood over her supine body. He didn't say anything at first, just scowled and sucked on his candy as he looked down at Bird. Then . . .

"That was fun."

"Um, what?" Bird released her breath.

"Working as a team." That was followed by the strangest sight of all: Mochabean grinned at her.

"Really?" Maybe there was something to this positive-thinking claptrap after all. "Glad you enjoyed it, big guy."

He held out his hand. Bird took it and got yanked up easy as you please. She was hit by a wave of nausea and had to hold onto Mochabean to steady herself. Then the vertigo passed and her legs solidified.

"Maybe we can do it again sometime," Mochabean said. "The team thing."

There had to be a few dozen reasons to say no—her head worked well enough to realize that, despite all the knocks it had recently taken—but for the life of her, Bird couldn't come up with a single one at the moment. And there was one extraordinarily compelling reason to say yes: Mochabean could easily crush them all under his size 16 boots at the moment. "Sure. You bet," Bird said.

"But next time I wanna be inside where the action is. No more of this backup business."

"Absolutely. You go inside, have yourself all the action you want. Me, I'll be outside with the pacifist collecting pixie sticks." She thumbed toward Jesse, whose pockets now bulged with candy treats.

Mochabean nodded in approval and grinned his scary grin.

Now steady on her feet, Bird helped Ruby to stand. The sisters leaned on each other for support.

"Bird, say I'd like to do this full-time. What kind of job benefits are we talking here: medical, dental, vacation?"

Ladybird Blacker took a detailed inventory of her surroundings:

Her pacifist partner Jesse skipped around the parking lot . . .

Mochabean, who was after their blood only days ago, now preferred the taste of a candy sucker in his mouth instead . . .

And perhaps most bizarre, her little sister, Ruby, who she feared would ruin her life but had instead saved it, stood next to Bird dressed in a clown suit as they helped each other stand.

With a tired grin, Bird admitted, "You know what? It's not such a bad job after all. You make your own hours, you don't work in an office . . . and you keep good company."

Some limping, some skipping, and some leaning on each other for support, the group shuffled off toward the van, and back to Da Vinci Bail Bonds.

19

MAN'S BEST FRIEND

BIRD WORE THE OLDEST, most worn-out clothes she had, scraped from somewhere in the back of her closet, when she returned to Harold Stiffe's house in Koreatown. It's not that she was trying to disguise herself. She was simply trying to protect the few good articles of clothing she had left. The past couple of weeks may have been hard on her, but they were hell on her garments—dog drool, gunshots, smoke grenades, explosions, her attire had been through it all. She'd come back to the Stiffe house, in fact, because she was running out of things to wear and remembered she had left one of her good ties there.

And as long as she was there she should probably release that thing trapped in the basement. She hoped the police had already taken care of the dog when the coroner came for Stiffe's body, so she wouldn't have to deal with the creature. But she knew her luck was never that good. Not so long ago, the dog had bitten off a chunk of her bulletproof vest and ruined one of her linen shirts before she managed to trap it in the home's basement. And then she was forced to leave behind her neckwear to secure the basement doorknob with it. The monster was probably still down there, hungry, and likely holding a grudge against her.

"God, I hope I don't die in this," she said, looking down at what she was wearing: lime-green sweatpants and a T-shirt with "Don't have a cow!" scrawled across the front. "Where on earth did I even get this?" she said and tugged on the ghastly shirt.

The front door of the home had police tape smattered all over it, warning people to not cross or, presumably, they would face the wrath of the LAPD. She ignored the bossy plastic strip and went inside, making a beeline for the basement door. Her tie was still secured around the doorknob on one end and tied to a table leg at the other, holding the door shut. You'd think the police would have noticed something like that when they were investigating the dead body. And perhaps they had. Maybe they ran across the gigantic dog and decided the best course of action was to leave it down in the basement and wait for animal control to handle it, only perhaps the dogcatcher got sidetracked somewhere along the way. Meanwhile, Bird was out one polyblend teal-colored tie with a charming goldfish accent she was rather fond of.

She quickly and quietly removed her neckwear from the door and turned to leave. Something nagged at her, however, something suspiciously close to guilt. Even if it had tried to kill her, the dog had now gone days without food or water down in the basement. She would have to be a complete ass to just leave it down there starving and thirsty.

She thought about it for a moment. "Fuck him, he tried to eat me." Turns out she had no problem being a complete ass.

Bird was almost to the front door when she heard the sounds, growling and ripping, followed by a miserable whine, all coming from the basement. Maybe the dog got so hungry down there that it was reduced to eating the dirty laundry. It was enough to put a dent in even her cast-iron heart. She couldn't leave the thing down there. "Guess I'm just a sucker for a hard case." She sighed.

Out of curiosity, Bird opened the kitchen fridge. All the food she found inside was an expired package of bacon, more of a clump than a package, really. The fridge also contained a couple of bottles of Mexican beer. She grabbed one for herself. "You owe me," she said to the heavens, addressing the dearly departed Harold Stiffe. Then she considered the sort of nefarious life Harold had chosen for himself and decided it would be more accurate to look downward when speaking to his ghost. "For all the trouble you and your dog put me through."

She returned to the basement door and took a long drink of beer to steel her resolve. She opened the door slowly, expecting to be attacked at any moment by the canine. When no slobbery attack was forthcoming, she opened it all the way and flicked on the light switch, which she was both surprised and thankful to find fully operational. The basement light flickered to life, but there was no sign of the dog, so Bird carefully walked down the creaking stairs. Again, she heard growling and ripping sounds.

"This better not get supernatural," she muttered. "Bad enough dealing with that ugly mutt without having to worry about haunted basements. Remember, I wasn't the one who shot you, Harry."

She reached the base of the stairs. Once there, she found the gigantic dog. It was in a corner of the room, chewing on the contents of a red gym bag.

"All right, dog, you don't like me and I won't pretend to like you," Bird said, legs slightly bent and ready to sprint out of there if necessary. "But I couldn't just leave you down here."

The dog looked up when it heard her voice. There were green bits in its mouth, as if it had been eating lettuce or some other vegetable. There was no such thing as a vegetarian dog, was there? Well, in Los Angeles perhaps, but she kept her distance from the beast just in case it still had a taste for flesh, specifically hers.

"I'm going to leave the door open, and you can go or stay, as you please. After that, I wash my hands of you."

Wait a second, that wasn't lettuce in the dog's mouth—last she checked, lettuce didn't carry portraits of dead presidents on it.

"Sweet Benjamin Franklin, it's money!" Bird reached out on impulse to stop the dog from destroying the cash. A sudden snap of the canine's jaws forced her to pull her hand back, grateful, however, that she still had all her fingers. But she couldn't let it chew up all that money; there must be twenty to thirty grand in that gym bag!

Remembering the clump of greasy bacon in the refrigerator, she got a brainstorm. "Tell you what, gruesome, you wait here, and I'll get you something far tastier than that grimy old money. What do you say?"

The beast cocked its head to the side thoughtfully. Did it understand her—was it actually considering the proposition? If so, it must not have liked the deal, as it immediately buried its snout back in the gym bag and tore apart another wad of cash, somewhere in the neighborhood of two grand by the looks of it.

"No!"

Bird sprinted back up the stairs and to the kitchen. She was back in less than thirty seconds, out of breath and with a handful of bacon in tow. The dog took no notice at first, content to munch away on what no doubt was the world's most expensive chew toy.

She waved the bacon around like a signal flare, trying to nab its attention. "Look here, ugly, I'll trade you this nice juicy, not-at-all-expired bacon for that filthy, filthy bag of useless money."

It hesitated only a moment, then caught a whiff of the fat-filled treat and galloped right at Bird, its huge tongue hanging out.

"Jeez!" She threw aside the bacon before the dog stampeded over her to get at it. The dog snapped it up off the floor and licked at the ground, making sure it got every last morsel. Meanwhile, Bird, who was shoving spilled money back into the gym bag, shook her head with pity. "Poor ignorant beast, a slave to your baser instincts."

Then Ladybird Blacker got down on hands and knees on the grimy basement floor and proceeded to collect every last scrap of shredded money she could get her hands on.